Shadows

of Chaos

BY

ANDREW LARKWOOD

BEYOND THE MIND,

KNOWLEDGE IS BOUNDLESS.

Shadows

of Chaos

COPYRIGHT © 2019, ANDREW LARKWOOD

Chapters

Chapter 1

The Light

"There is no true divide between men other than a perception of what is seen as true. You must learn to take good moral value from religion and proven fact from science together in order to know the balance of what you see." Maya's father told her at the beginning of a chat which would forever alter her perception of reality.

"Mistakes are inevitable," he added, while glancing off toward the horizon, "mistakes are actions which fail your predicted outcome and beg for you to rectify, until either your mind forgets or a solution is found. Rarely are sustained solutions found, but they do exist. Your achievements will be short, though immensely impactful, sparing you little time to fester in success."

Maya uses eye contact to emphasize her words, show respect, and relate to how others are feeling. Jack's use of eye contact is similar, except he has a chilling way of pushing words through someone with a dead and fearless stare.

For the majority of her conscious life, Maya struggled with exclusion, which she grew to accept as "just the way things are for most people on the planet" like an inevitable consequence of living. Despite feeling indifferent and disconnected from others, she actively and intentionally suppressed related emotion with a belief she didn't know the entire story; how true it would become.

"I don't know the half of it," Maya would tell her mind time and time again in attempt to keep sane through life's misfortunes.

Jack's use of direct eye contact happened only a few short times during his one-sided conversation with Maya. From the beginning of the chat, Maya recognized her father's words were a precursor to a much larger and more significant point to come.

When he's on a roll like this, Maya prefers to listen and learn, and let Jack say everything he needs to. Maya understands he loves to think out loud and sort thoughts during conversation. Plus, knowing the conversation could easily turn into a bombardment of tangents, she didn't want to interrupt him for her own sanity.

He has a distinct ability to control an entire conversation using passionate words paired with calculating eyes as keen as a career detective. The effectiveness of his conversational tactics is barely blunted by frequent use and he always finds a way to pull someone into it like a flytrap.

Maya and her father rested at an old picnic table partway up a mountain which overlooks a valley with rolling hills covered by dense forest. The wind was breezy and cool on a humid day with just enough static in the air to tingle nasal hairs. It's a pleasant day, free from signs of foul weather and the like; a reminder of times in a meadow from Maya's early years.

"Eventually, there is a time when a father must pass along his wisdom, and for me, well there is more to include, Maya." He said to her. "It is time for you to see what I see and to know what I know. It's time for me to pass along the greatest responsibility the world may never know."

To explain Maya's father, Jack Kaona, as old and wise is an understatement of his character. He lived a long and healthy life up until this point, with surprisingly no physical complications for his age. One might regard his health as a winner of a genetic lottery of sorts; at least this is true as an outsider looking in.

As his daughter, Maya closely witnessed Jack from a different perspective than outsiders would have it. She noticed his persistence and an uncanny ability to shake off stress while remaining calm under fire. Perhaps that is why those who are closer to him sometimes refer to him as Laid-Back Jack in passing.

He is a brisk man with a dark complexion and a fit body from years of manual labor working with machinery. There are few men as charismatic considering life pushed him in many directions, at times beyond thresholds others wouldn't dare cross. Jack confronts adversity as a precipice to scale and conquer. Trustworthy and honesty are synonymous with his outlook on life.

"This changes everything you know about everything that is or will ever be. The universe is not quite as it seems and it does not really fit into what people on Earth have made it out to be. They are influenced by a force beyond comprehension to most."

The deep and meaningful has taken a turn into the cryptic and conspiratorial. Except when talking with Jack, conspiracy is too far removed from good moral of spirituality and scientific fact.

"Beyond comprehension of most, what do you mean?" Maya quipped.

"I'm tired of sitting, let's go for a walk." He responded.

They followed a winding path up an incline toward a clearing in the distance. Greenery on either side of the path soon parted and they were standing on a large flat rock plateau leading to a sheer cliff drop-off into the valley below.

"This is the place, Maya; this is where my part in the world you know started." He said while subtly trying to catch a breath. "There is a story I must tell you, but unfortunately I won't be able to tell you all of it."

Jack turned around from looking towards the valley and proceeded to slowly sit on a rocky outcrop. Faint beads of sweat were forming on his cheeks and forehead. He seemed to struggle a little while trying to gain his composure.

Maya found her father's duress somewhat unusual considering the walk wouldn't normally disconcert him; at least in an obvious way. He pulled a small checkered cloth from his pocket, lightly dabbed his forehead, and then began his story.

"Many years ago, long before your mother and I met, I experienced what you could call my first significant epiphany. It was definitely an epiphany because I felt enlightenment like never before." He nervously lightly clears his throat and continues.

Maya glanced at her father's profile as he pivoted to look at the horizon again. With age, his hair migrated from dark brown to silver and gray while maintaining' a pronounced wave pattern. Instead of trying to hide the gray, he embraces it as a badge of honor. The silver hairs shimmered in the sunlight like a smelt shoal agitated by a school of salmon.

"I went out with friends one night only to end up walking home alone. It wasn't a long way, but it was a fair distance and I decided to make an adventure out of it by walking down the center of an abandoned railroad track with a flask and a little smoke."

He enjoys endurance walking and wouldn't have trouble walking those same railroad tracks today as he did way back when. Though rough around the edges, Jack's bristles and wrinkles are testaments to a life busy, wise, and weathered; in a good way.

Maya thought, "Oh here we go. It's a story from his golden days again."

She heard plenty of her father's stories over the years and enough to know he wasn't shy about enlightening substances. The thing Maya didn't understand though is what brought him to a life of reclusion after the fact, and something about the conversation made Maya think she was about to find out.

Jack continued his talk, "I asked myself the question, is it possible for people to predict the future and what is the implication if so? Further questions spawned from this, it literally consumed my thoughts for years. Then one day, and a lifetime of knowledge later, on this very plateau I found an answer."

Deep down, he understands the need for rolling up his sleeves to get the job done. In the eyes of Maya's father, there are no lengths too far, within a positive moral framework, for learning, knowledge, and understanding.

"Do you see the trees, way over there in the distance?" he pauses for a second and waves his arm in a half-circle, pointing across the distant tree tops.

"From way back here, the trees create an appealing pattern, but the closer you get the more detailed that pattern becomes. What may appear uniform from here looks more and more random the closer you get. What I learned is, those trees are part of recursive mathematical function." He pointed out before continuing on with increasing enthusiasm.

"The same recursive mathematical function is shared by plants around the world, right down to the microscopic level. Part of the pattern is found in DNA and switches which determine how each plant will grow and look. The other part is a collection of environmental factors which work together in stimulating the plant by restricting or encouraging prosperity."

Maya asked inquisitively, "You're telling me, science is too focused on the forest instead of what makes up the trees?"

"In some respects, but it's not a matter of being too focused on the forest when plenty study the trees too. It's the fact that in a lot of cases, those focused on only trees do not understand the forest from their perspective, and vice versa." He responded.

"Think of those systems," Jack continued.

"All involved material is affected by all mass in contact with it and their environments. It's a level of recursion too, though not quite bold, like stating falling rain in Northern Asia creates a flood in South America. My point, is that until we can trace the life of a raindrop across the planet, who can prove it doesn't?"

Maya didn't know how to handle the point and shrugged with a sideways nod.

"Now imagine a vast number of elements in a single system, and their countless influential factors on other systems, it's a form of infinite probability of influence. An example, each of those pine trees over there shed needles and cones on a biological schedule specific to their species."

An evident level of giddiness finds a way into his voice, like he's laughing at the punchline of his own joke. "Can you tell me where each one will land?"

"On the ground in a pile at the base of the tree, gravity pulls objects to the ground," Maya replied with an obvious influential factor.

"Certainly," he said, "gravity does affect the system, but there are many other factors as well. Ultimately, each shed needle and cone may end up on the ground, or stuck on a branch below from where it fell, or carried away to make a bird nest somewhere."

Maya looked surprised, knowing now she unintentionally took a forest-type standpoint by noting gravitational pull instead of a tree-type standpoint by looking at environmental influence on the pine needles.

Her father adds to her surprise by saying, "What if I told you I can pinpoint each and every location those leaves would land? What if we could predict the exact final resting place for each needle and cone to a precise location?"

This sounded quite impossible to Maya. She replied, "What kind of crazy technology is needed to track millions of pine needles, aggregate the data with environmental conditions, and then use it in a meaningful way to predict the outcome?

Jack started grinning like he knew how.

Maya paused for a moment. After noticing her father's smile, she added, "Then you'd be an absolute genius. Such a discovery is unparalleled and a revelation without any known limitation."

"Correct!" He claimed with an emphatic smile. "I wouldn't go so far as to state I'm a genius, but I did figure something out there is at least one known limitation discovered – that is why we're here today."

Maya was caught off-guard in a transitional phase between fantasy and reality. She interjected before her father had a chance to continue, "Wait a minute, if you figured out there is a limitation then that means you discovered the solution to chaotic theory – you can see time."

"You're right and it's incredible, Maya." He paused, looked out at the trees and hills again, and then back at Maya.

"I spent years looking for the unfathomable line which best describes an unpredictable curve; through many trials, experiments, and times of grief. During those years, my feelings were like up and down gravitational forces I've experienced on rollercoasters, but with a lot of determination, I managed to find the curve itself."

Maya thought, "This is astounding and practically unbelievable."

In all the time she spent with her father, and everything she understands about the reality of existence itself, he lays claim something of this magnitude? She has doubts on a scientific level and now wonders if her father has lost his mind or if he trying to test her credulity.

"Forgive me if I sound a little skeptical, but what do you mean by finding the curve itself?" Maya asked.

Before her father could answer, she added, "If I were to jump off a bridge in a leap of faith, there would have to be some water below, and even better with a bungee cord."

A look of solemnity suffused over Jack's face while he adjusted his posture into something more appropriate for confiding. "Maya, a leap of faith means jumping into the unknown; your faith will see you through it. There won't always be a safety net and sometimes you just have to trust in yourself."

Maya cowered a little bit over how deep her father could be, and knowing her analogy wasn't the best choice for how she felt about chaotic theory's mysteries.

"Anyway, this is more than a leap of faith; it is a bound of knowledge." He stated, and then took yet another pause before continuing.

Jack uses verbal pauses for emphasis, but the silence can be disruptive to his thoughts; usually because a delay in thought directs his mind to a completely different train of thought without hesitation. Jack often needs a moment to find his way back to the subject at hand when his mind wanders.

"For you to learn more is commitment to the responsibility of this knowledge. You must understand the place forward from here is exactly why I began spending the great majority of my time away from public interaction. This is serious, dangerous, thrilling, and previously undiscovered information capable of hiding you away."

Many strangely curious questions popped into Maya's head at that instant. The thoughts battered around like tennis balls in clothes dryer. She couldn't sort all of them out right away and figured it's best to remain silent for the time being. Right now, she is walking a hypothetical edge, thinking her father is either a genius or has lost it completely.

"Thunk, thu-thunk. Thunk." Maya pictured the low resonating sound tennis balls tumbling on a fluff cycle and smiled a little. It looks as though Maya also had the tendency to allow her mind to wander in thoughts mid-sentence.

Jack looked at Maya in a way of knowing she was struggling with credibility on the subject, to which he responded, "If you cannot commit to the responsibility of knowledge then we'll have to scratch the notion and blame this as me losing my mind. Trust me; you want to commit to this for the coordinates of your future." He said with another ecstatic grin.

"Normally time would help me weigh such a large decision." Maya replied.

Jack didn't believe his own daughter would try using time as an excuse. He remained silent and glared at her a little bit.

She replied and looked around at the rocky escarpment, "I'll do my best to understand and anything we talk about is between you, me, and these rocks."

"Very well," he responded.

"You will have to learn to function and live from shadows you create. This is necessary for survival because the solution to chaotic theory gives enough power to make you a threat to every country in the world."

Her father went from a light-hearted, ever-smiling presence to a look serious enough to cut glass. The pitch of his voice dampened to match.

"I have been living as far under the radar as possible since the discovery and only make outside contact when my calculations allow for it. This is only the beginning, a cornerstone if you will. What you learn with this knowledge unlocks many other doors and may one day lead to the keystone."

Jack walked over to the cliff and turned to face Maya while changing the conversation.

"You shouldn't continue beating yourself up for what happened to your mother." He said.

"Things don't always work out the way we want them to. While it may not make sense at the time, you'll find truth when you're meant to know it."

Maya felt crushing sadness over the loss of her mother as thoughts of the past raced through her mind. She remembered being vividly upset and blamed herself as Jack noted. What happened wasn't her fault, but for some reason Maya felt like she could have prevented it.

Her father's words brought tears of mixed emotion. The freakish accident, which looked like foul play, still doesn't make sense to Maya or her father. Maya could not think of any reason why someone would go after her mother. While the mystery of her death points to a case of being at the wrong place at the wrong time, Maya couldn't help but believe it was a consequence of something she did unknowingly.

By this time the sun was going down into the trees, pouring a mixture of light across the valley below like a giant placed a prism on the horizon, reflecting pink, red, orange and yellow blends into the sky and over the forest landscape.

Maya looked at the beautiful sunset while thinking about how the dazzling array of colors reminded her of her mother's vibrance, fading into blackness as the sun disappeared. She pressed her lips together and scrunched her eyebrows closer in a subconscious effort to mask the pain.

"It is time for me to move on, too." He said.

Jack added to the thought before Maya had a chance to realize what he just said, "Remember this also, your mother and I will always be with you. Anywhere you travel with the Kaona name entwined, there will always be a way out nearby. Your fingers are keys to transportation and not a single soul on Earth has your pattern."

"What do you mean, move on, too? Where are you going?" Maya asked.

Jack dodged Maya's questions and replied, "If the end justifies the means, how does death justify life?"

He paused for a moment as Maya grappled with the question and then continued his thought, "I planned for every second tonight and where you need to be next. Take this flash drive, proceed to your first destination, and I will meet up with you again."

He glanced at the mountain, back at Maya, and lobbed a memory card in her direction.

"You will understand everything from the cave on the mountain; and remember this, go north and east first, Maya."

Maya was confused and wasn't sure what to say next, plus she had to jump to pluck the flash drive from the air. Simultaneously, at the moment she was reaching for the flash drive, her father gracefully leapt backwards over the cliff.

Maya ran over to the edge in complete disbelief of what just happened – she desperately tried to contain her fear.

He father fell through the air while looking up at the heavens with a content smile on his face.

"Is this his leap of faith, or him trying to find out how death justifies life?" Maya thought.

Seconds later, suddenly, Jack transformed into a glowing effervescent sphere of blue light midway through his fall. The pulsating object split into several small rays before passing through the valley as thin streaks of bright blue light gradually blend into the sunset.

Like gift box ribbons flowing in the wind, the blue light streaks wrapped around a mountain in the distance and shot upward into space – all of which took place within a few seconds, and for Maya, it felt like time slowing into eternity.

***

Each day in the valley, hikers traverse a public recreational trail in the forest as a favored scenic activity in the area. Several paths slice through aging vegetation, moss-covered outcrops, and over run-off streams in a genuinely rustic setting. Hiking the trails here is a promise to adventurers of seclusion as they witness the truly wild environment; and, there's an added bonus today.

A group of four hikers planned to complete the entire seven-mile outer valley loop before dusk after arriving at the trailhead around lunch time. Provided they kept pace, completing the loop is a likely possibility, even if the last hour happens to turn into a night hike.

Though today's hike is casual, it's also part of an endurance practice for the group. They share a common belief of being prepared for a doomsday event by always carrying survival supplies, placing food and water caches, and maintaining multiple escape routes from populated areas.

The weather forecast predicts mostly clear skies into early morning hours with zero percent change of precipitation. In a timely waxing phase, the moon would provide extra light for anyone still traveling during later hours. Daytime temperature is in the mid-seventies, cooling into the fifties by early morning.

Partially maintained paths branch off the main loop into exploratory sections of the valley. The primary trail has blue circle markers for a throughway to a thousand-mile backpacking trail running along the entire mountain range. White blazes on trees mark the main loop to help with navigation through dense forest areas.

Earlier on, about half an hour before the group of hikers left, Maya and her father parked at the trail head and then walked around two miles down the main loop to an offshoot trail subtly identified by a small triangle carving in the bark of a nearby tree.

Maya and Jack followed the short, winding path to a marshy clearing surrounded by trees and shrubs. The narrow path picked up on the other side, which is also marked by a carved triangle on a tree due to potential overgrowth. The path curved up a hill to another clearing with a rocky overlook and plateau.

The group of four hikers is composed of two women and two men who are adults in their mid-thirties. They are long-time platonic friends, Kara, Kelly, Brad, and Paul. Everyone anticipated completing the entire loop by late afternoon and managed to traverse a lot of ground effortlessly within a few short hours; trail times are logged by Paul for later assessment.

Once in a while, casual banter broke long bouts of silence as they trekked forward. Making a little noise at times is how each member of the group kept track of each other. Like a tiny network of computers sending keep-alive pings, the chatter lets other machines know they're still online.

The hikers are thoughtful, kindred souls who share a tireless affinity for the outdoors. They hiked together many times in the past, with a few journeys along the main loop, and feel confident in their knowledge of the terrain.

Half-way through the day, nearing mile number four of the hike, the group crossed paths with an older man walking an old black lab. The strange man kept to himself while heading in an opposite direction of the group.

The four friends easily remembered hiker's etiquette, which is a conditioned behavior from years of meeting people on trails, and politely said hello to the odd man. He didn't respond verbally and instead cast a nod and forced smile in the general direction of the group. The black Labrador walked ahead of him, panting a little, staring into the woods without breaking focus.

After passing the unknown man, Kelly took a look behind her to see if he was gone and then said in a low voice with slight on her lips, "He's an odd one, eh?"

Kelly is an interesting person who easily appeals to both sexes with a knack for reminding people of someone they must have met before. She is attractive looking with unique characteristics in her eyes and nose. Her personality is wholesome and bright as a person who enjoys helping others. She is hardly afraid to ask for help or approach strangers for casual talk.

Paul felt similar and glanced at Kelly to say, "Yea he is, and did you see the dog?"

Kelly replied, "Staring off into the forest abyss like something is not right in the head."

Discombobulated and cute, is how people often describe Paul to others. He knows his smartass persona surfaces easily and attempts to suppress how he truly feels to keep the peace, but he is not able to hide it well enough. He has an evolving crush on Kelly and this is an opportune moment to flirt.

Paul grinned and said, "Both of them were creepy if you ask me. I've heard people say dogs are reflections of their owners and I bet that man has a few screws loose like his dog."

Kelly lightly laughed at Paul's comments by finding humor in how he said it more than what he said.

Two hours of hiking pass since running into the old man and his dog. Casual chatter kept the group pleasantly entertained. When near the end of the trail, Kara was suddenly enamored by a glimmer of blue light above the trees she caught in the corner of her left eye.

"Guys, look at that! Holy crap! Do you see it?" Kara said while extending her arm to point at the moving ball of light.

Those who understand Kara are aware her personality tends to lead with a childish side, but she drops the jesting act quickly if more serious matters arise. She is very outgoing and sometimes too flirty for her own good. Her close friends have addressed the flirtation with her a few times and have realized she is a natural flirt who isn't able to switch it off.

"Hey, I'm not a guy." Kelly quipped with a snarky remark, and then stuck her tongue out to tease.

Brad stopped, looked at Kara for a second like a delayed reaction of hearing her voice, and turned in the direction she was pointing.

"Holy, what in the heck," He said with an emphatic inflection.

An all-around nice guy, Brad is the man a father would be proud to have as a son. Despite the theory of girls only liking bad boys, Brad has found girls are naturally fond of him. He tends to act older than he really is and his looks back it up. Brad's maturity shines through and girls recognize it as a good quality they want in their life, though he tends to ruin it sometimes with silly jokes.

Paul chimed in with his eyebrows uneasily wrinkled up into his forehead, "Is this for real?"

The ball of blue light rapidly moved closer to the tree tops above the hikers. Before hitting the trees, the orb dispersed into narrow strands and spread across the canopy.

"Was that really an UFO?" Kara asked.

"I don't know. If so, you would say a UFO, not an UFO – Maybe they already got you, Kara." Kelly replied with a laugh.

"Wait, what? How rude do you need to be, Kelly? See, I can be rude too, but I won't because it's not nice to be a mean person." Kara responded. "I spoke too fast, you know, because of an insane, fracking flying UFO."

Kelly was distracted by the object too, but felt it would be more fun to antagonize Kara over her slip-up.

"Well, it sounds good to use 'an' before 'unidentified', but it doesn't sound proper with 'an' acronym." Kelly said while using air-quotes with her fingers.

Kara replies after sticking out her tongue again, "Still not a guy and your air-quotes are so third grade."

Brad jumped in. "Would you two children knock it off for a minute? Whatever it was, I don't think we should be sticking around, arguing about grammar, to find out. It's getting dark and maybe it was just lightning or something. Kara should lay off eating random mushrooms off the trail and getting us all paranoid."

Paul laughed at Brad and joined the tease by adding his two cents to the conversation. "He's right, let's get out of here. It was probably a flying fungus. We've been hiking for the last five hours with only water and hardly any food."

He then whispers under his breath, causing Brad to laugh at the notion, "I don't know why I said a flying fungus, it just came out. Did she really eat trail mushrooms?"

Brad shook his head from side to side, "We better get going."

The group continued hiking for a few more minutes until the parking lot came into view and stopped for a moment to assess their performance. Conditioning from long hikes weekly is starting to pay off and they can cover a lot of ground quickly with little resources.

Paul stopped the group to announce their timing today, "Hey folks, guess what? We finished twenty minutes faster than last time. Granted, we were delayed then by Kara's bruised ankle from stepping in a hole."

Kelly replied, "Awesome! I think last week was good practice too, we were able to finish out the hike and knew how to handle Kara's injury."

"Sorry about that, but it was a pitfall, there were leaves and twigs covering the hole," Kara said while feeling guilty for holding up the group then.

Brad addressed Kara's mishap too, "Hey, it wasn't your fault and like Kelly said, we overcame that together which prepares us for similar events. It can get much worse if there are hostiles in the area, and no emergency services for miles."

Chapter 2

Station Seven

A few minutes after her father jumped into the valley, Maya hiked down the hillside from the lookout to the main trail. Instead of heading back to the parking lot, she follows the trail north toward an obscured path branching off the top of the loop per directions from her father.

By now it's dark in the forest and spotting a hidden path is more difficult. Maya is carrying a tactical pack with numerous survival tools which are especially useful for the task. She grabs a compact, high-intensity UV black light flashlight from a side pocket and flips it on.

Shining the spotlight at trees ahead will illuminate a triangle insignia stamped in a glowing phosphorescent resin; likewise, the beam does not create a beacon visible in the distance to attract unwanted attention. This is an ingenious idea her father came up with after getting lost in the woods once while looking for the same trail many years ago.

Maya recalls when she was younger and how Jack would take her hiking in the same forest. He tirelessly fostered an interest and appreciation for the outdoors using cryptology with puzzles to solve along the way. He also emphasized survival, self-sufficiency, and methods for remaining calm under fire.

A phrase of his tireless advice stuck out in her mind, "Panic is at the heart of all irrational decisions."

After spotting a triangle, Maya follows this path up the side of the mountain until it narrows into nothingness. The diminishing path relies on overgrowth masking direction from here forward and it's entirely up to the hiker to know which way they're going.

The vegetation is slightly damp from late evening dew. Sounds of katydids and crickets in harmony fill the mild air along with an occasional deep wood's owl hoot. Bull frogs in nearby marshy areas add to the orchestra with resonating songs much like plucking thick rubber bands at random.

To help with navigation in the dark, Maya has a phosphorescent-lined compass. Shining UV light on the compass for a few seconds charges small phosphorescent markings on the face for better visibility without light. After a few moments following the compass, she reaches a rocky plateau similar to the overlook on the other side of the valley.

Her flashlight picked up an unusual object at this point. For an unexplainable reason, Maya stumbled across a trail camera which is likely not her father's handy work. Maya approached it and unclipped the latches to flip the camera open. She pulled out a memory card and AA batteries from the housing and put them in her backpack. With any luck, she might be able to see who placed it by looking at the first few stills.

On the other side of the plateau, where the camera was pointing towards, Maya discovers a cavern carved into the rock. The cavern resembles a natural void which was expanded to create a deeper chamber; unless someone took the time to blast loads of hard rock out of the way.

An old rusty wrought iron gate covered in creeping ivy and dense moss blocks the entrance, but it is not secured shut by a lock. The uniquely designed gate, with twisted spindles and sweeping curves, is controlled by a biometric sensor to operate a hydraulic opening mechanism.

Maya is spooked by the sound of rustling leaves and twig snaps near the path she followed up the mountain. It sounded like an animal, but she couldn't tell for sure. She froze in place and waited to hear the noises again as ambient forest sounds picked up where they left off. Frog croaks refilled the air loudly, followed by the katydids as before, like her ears focused away and now hear them for the first time.

A few fireflies whirl in a light breeze.

"What was that?" She whispered.

Not interested in spending any more time waiting around to find out what she heard, Maya locates a biosensor with her black light, pops the lid upwards and places her right ring finger on a pressure pad to open. The gate slides down into a void inside the plateau, she jumps in the cave, and the gate stays open for seven seconds before automatically closing itself.

"Here we are." She says, as her bottom lip nervously quivering while standing in the dark for a moment.

Lights along the floor turn on to trace a hallway contour as the gate closed. Two cobbled stone walls jetting out from the sides create a maze-like foyer to block light from going outside.

Maya walked into the maze section and the contour lights turned off. Beyond the maze walls, now lit from a motion sensor, is a wider room about twice as wide as the entrance. The central room contains three open entrances, with a single doorway on each wall. Old barn wood appears to be holding up the doorways like support structures in a mining cave.

The hidden cavern area is a mountain lab her father built and nicknamed Station Seven. It is also nautically themed, orientated with Cardinal Directions and resembles the captain's quarters of a wooden ship. Jack's interior decorating, which may have indicated he spent a lot of time there, helps mask the otherwise drab, cold and heartless cavern.

Dimly lit by flickering ornate sconces, one located above each door, the central room has an appealing atmosphere. A writing desk and chair sit next to the western wall. On the eastern wall hangs a small wooden-pegged coat rack with a shoe rack directly on the floor below. Covering the floor is a unique area rug with a navy-blue Compass Rose pointing an arrow at each room on its dial.

Through the eastern doorway is a power room containing three battery arrays stacked side by side, each one as tall as a fridge. Thick wiring is bolted to the wall behind the battery array, which feeds a control panel distributing power to the other rooms. A small turbine generator system, fixed into a corner has a pump and evaporator attached to a large diameter pipe running directly into the floor.

There are two power sources feeding the battery array, the primary and auxiliary. Discretely placed solar panels outside provide power to the auxiliary system over a feeder line, which acts as the pump ignition and a low-power backup.

The primary system pumps spring water from below the cavern, through an evaporator, turbine, and power generator to create geothermal energy. Hot water also circulates through pipes to each of the rooms as an exchanger system to help moderate indoor climate.

Across the hall, in the western room, is a handcrafted workbench stocked with electronics and tools. Two laptops, placed on the left side, are networked to a server sitting below the bench. An oscilloscope, radio antenna, and weather station are hooked up to the laptops, with a seismic sensor connected to the server.

Wiring runs behind the bench and through a conduit in the stone wall. Outside, the wiring is buried a few inches deep as it snakes toward a set of trees not far from the cave. A large antenna is fixed to a pine tree trunk and cleverly camouflaged to blend into the branches. Further up the tree are components of the weather station.

The northern room, by far the coziest one in the lab, is the sleeping quarters. A plush double bed with a handcrafted frame, several blankets over the mattress and a set of pillows, is especially inviting after a long day of hiking. Apparently, her father invested a lot of time in building the cavern and Maya is especially thankful for the effort as she sits down on the bed.

At the foot of the bed is a wooden chest for clothes, extra blankets and sheets. A food pantry stands against the other wall, stocked with enough rations and water to last a month if need be. In the northern room, there is a faint smell of old wood in the air which somehow overpowers the stagnant mildew aroma of the cave.

Before turning in for the night, Maya went to the western room, powered up a laptop, and dropped the backpack beside a chair.

"Let's see what's on this." She said while plugging in the drive Jack lobbed before jumping into the valley.

After a fingerprint scan, access to disk contents didn't reveal an immediate answer, but instead directed her to a clue. Only one decrypted file, labelled S7.txt, showed up in the file browser. It contained a sequence of numbers, 38513538, on a single line.

"This is interesting. Is it a combination of some sort or a numeric pass code perhaps?" Maya thought. "Why would my father give me a flash drive that only has a series of eight numbers?"

Curious about the trail camera card, Maya decided to check out its contents too. The idea of it being a Trojan crossed her mind and she scanned the card first before browsing. There were several pictures of deer grazing on the wide angle from a different location, but nothing showing the cavern. One picture caught a blurry linear object, which looks a lot like an arm waved in front of the lens.

Her thoughts continued. "Maybe I'm too tired right now." She said with a sigh. Instead of getting too flustered over the numbers, Maya went to the north room to sleep.

While lying in bed, she thought about the day's crazy events, while staring at the ceiling, and couldn't quite understand if what happened really did.

Then she thought of one of the last things her father said before giving her the flash drive. "You'll want to commit to this for the coordinates of your future."

She sprung up from the bed and blurted out, "Coordinates, of course!"

Maya ran back to the workbench to grab a handheld GPS from her tactical bag. The very last thing her father said was also cryptic, in which he stated north and east first. She put clues together to arrive at coordinates of 38° 51'N 35° 38'E, and entered them into her GPS handheld.

"Unbelievable!" She said.

The coordinates point to Ash Hill, known as Kültepe, in Turkey. Fearing that she would forget the coordinates if her GPS died, or she lost her portable drive, Maya took a piece of paper and pencil off the desk and wrote them down as backup.

This is a famed archaeological site where tens of thousands of cuneiform tablets have been discovered over the years. Cuneiform was invented by the Sumerians and is regarded as one of the first known written languages to exist on Earth. For her father to leave her a clue as what is considered by many as the first written language, this is profound evidence there is much more to come.

Now beyond tired, Maya took to the north room once again to sleep. This time she fell into a deep slumber rather quickly and was plainly too tired, both physically and mentally, for thoughts to prevent it any longer. The peaceful rest was very much overdue, almost as much as the comfortable warm bed in a quiet, secluded hideaway.

***

The unknown man, passed by hikers earlier in the day, fumbles around outside of the cavern. It appears he is attempting to find out where Maya went after watching her traverse the path up to the cave plateau; his dog, hot on the trail of Maya's scent, leads the way.

This scenario is one Jack accounted for when he built the hideout, and a key reason why he went to extra lengths in camouflage detail and with using biometric security to keep it hidden. The man left after a few minutes; possibly thinking it would be easier to spot something in daylight, or perhaps after finding out his trail camera had been emptied.

Seven hours later Maya woke up refreshed and revitalized; she was confused for a moment trying to remember where she was. Thoughts from the day before flooded back to her like water rushing over rapids on the Colorado River; today her next adventure begins. After changing, she went into the west room in search of additional information.

While briefly looking around again, Maya spots a HAM radio, with an orange bar dialed to an unknown frequency, sitting on the right side of the workbench. All of the frequency labels on the radio have been scratched off from overuse or perhaps intentionally for some reason.

A microphone on a self-supporting stand is hooked up to the second laptop and faces into the radio's speaker. An audio cable connects the computer's audio jack to the radio microphone port, allowing the computer to receive and send transmissions.

Suddenly there are air pops, crackles, and static noises emanating from the radio speaker. Shortly after this, a series of rapid tones varying in pitch fill the air like an old dial-up modem.

The listening laptop's screen flips on from a blank screensaver, and a terminal window pops up. It translates the message into text as "Station-2 is nominal." A cursor slowly blinks at the end of this line.

Message two arrives a few seconds after, "Station-3 is degraded with low power alert. Then another transmission stating "Station-4 is nominal with seal intact."

Again, another message next, "Station-5 is nominal." Followed quickly by a message stating, "Station-6 is nominal."

Seconds pass by with the sound of white noise, and then a single tone plays for one second; this is an update beacon. The console window prompts a message, "Station-7 is nominal."

The transmit signal is not heard, since it plays directly into the radio microphone port. A follow-up message also plays into the port with a series of status messages letting other stations know it received their transmissions.

This system of encrypted communication works like an Enigma machine, but instead uses a computer to encode and decode the message. It's capable, when programmed, to update stations without wireless networks or the internet.

"Now this is a fascinating system, and with a pulse!" She said while turning towards the other laptop.

The computer and server both require two-step validations; fingerprint identification and a tokenized USB key for access. After verification on the laptop, Maya opened an itinerary spreadsheet from the desktop, as left by her father.

Information on the sheet details Station-6 location and its importance to her father's chaotic theory discovery. In fact, the first half of the code can be found at Station-6 along with details on how to complete it.

She thought about needing to arrive there without drawing much attention. Leaving a parked vehicle is out of the question, which reminds her of the car still parked at the trailhead a few miles away.

Details on the document continue to reveal the degraded low power alert reported by Station-3 is intentional as a decoy. This antenna is hooked to a utility pole with a signal emitter disguised as a telephone junction box, in the middle of nowhere, not far from a remote switching station.

It's a long-forgotten part of the power grid once installed for housing development project, which is now defunct, and oddly enough the utility company hasn't cut power after years of disrepair.

Further notes identify last minute supplies, directions to Station-6, and a cash stash in the northern room. Of all places and creative ideas, he could conceive, her father lined a garment bag with cash and hid it under the mattress. This held true to her father's basic attitude about cash; a necessary ticket in this world but not the most important thing.

"Here I thought the crinkling plastic noise every time I moved was a moisture barrier." Maya joked. "Retrieval won't be too bad then, I guess."

Which ironically, she later struggled with, as a fabric loop on the garment bag snagged on a bent nail, making not as easy as it sounded to remove.

After that fiasco, she emptied the suit bag, placed most of the cash in the tactical pack, and then tucked a few bills into her front right jean pocket.

Final points in the document discuss exit protocol. Leaving the hideaway means burying the cavern with a remote detonation after arming a payload. All of the hard work put into building this place was entirely to serve the purpose it has, and now it would be lost to history.

Reading that became a defining moment and it clearly put into perspective exactly what's at stake here, as if she required further convincing. In basic principal, she must consciously keep her identity concealed and tracks covered.

Maya proceeded to follow the exit details, first by checking a camera with eyes outside of the cavern gate. She pockets the flash drive her father gave her, and places a handheld GPS and long-range radio transmitter in the tactical sack.

Next up, she pushes a trigger on each box, designed to overload circuits, to destroy memory on the solid-state drives. With the smell of burning electronics, and smoke exiting the computers, the overload appeared to work nicely.

Then she cranks open steam release valves in the west, central hallway, and north rooms. Mist fills the air as she runs into the east room and opens a bypass on the geothermal intake pipe; hot water streams along the pipes and begins pooling on the floor around the valves. Flipping the bypass also enabled a remote radio trigger hooked up to the battery array.

With all measures in place, Maya opens the wrought iron gate, whispers "we're in mission-mode now," and leaves the cavern.

After a brisk hike through the woods, and down the divergent path, Maya makes her way to the main loop and back to the trailhead. By this time, around one o'clock, two inches of water cover the cave floor and a fine water mist coats nearly every visible surface.

Now she has a narrow view of the cavern rock face location from the car a few miles away. With the car started and ready to go, Maya pulls a rocker switch on her handheld.

It took a few long seconds for the array to ignite as the radio signal activated a sparking mechanism. A small plume of smoke, which really looked like a campfire from a distance, then puffed into the sky above.

In the instant Maya drove away, a peculiar and odd thing happened, the cavern area affected by flooding and implosion suddenly appeared to melt. The whole cavern transformed into rocks and foliage that blended into the mountainside.

Chapter 3

Distant Horizon

Maya is just over five feet tall with a lovely appeal which most sensible men consider pleasant on the visual cortex. A deeper personality stirs below the surface, though. She is fixated on utility over vanity and believes too much emphasis on glamor detracts from beauty within. Ironically, to some, it's even more bewitching to find a woman as fascinating on multiple levels.

She prefers a chameleon-like approach to life and its situations, priding moderation, and an ability to adapt to changing environments. For the majority of her life, Maya has worked diligently in building a diverse skill set which she considers to be an inviolable toolkit.

Her hair is shoulder length, wavy, and dark blond with golden highlights throughout her bangs. She generally likes to keep her hair back in a band, pulled out of the way for concentration, but will occasionally let it down to let her follicles relax.

Attributing to Maya's inherited practical, yet subversive personality, she usually wears light makeup no jewelry. She sometimes uses eyeliner and eyeshadow for formal affairs, as a connection to her seriousness more so than for its attractive quality. A similar approach is made in style with preference to casual and comfortable Earth tones as opposed to bright, dressy, or restrictive fashion.

Being prepared for unknowns is a passion fused to who Maya really is, but it can also be an ailment of progress. An example of this, which developed over many years, strives to consider as many possible outcomes as humanly conceivable. Over-weighing tough decisions, or even simplistic ones, leads to a hesitation over matters.

While some may consider Maya's thinking habits as peculiar and self-destructive, those same thoughts allow her to visually imagine a level of quantum mechanics applied to her world on a daily basis. With a lot of practice, and patience, the effort needed to do this dwindled into a fine point of almost nothingness; and now, strategic thinking at a quantum level is second nature to Maya.

Thinking at this level also takes a toll on emotional response. Her thought process creates a struggle between feelings and facts, which can become both tormenting and enlightening in the same breath. To help counteract this struggle, and maintain her sanity, Maya spends time with her emotions in similar ways.

Through tantric exercises reminiscent of obsessive-compulsive disorder, Maya unknowingly created a telepathic bridge between the spiritual realm of existence, with the Celestial Council, and the scientific world around her.

For conscious people on Earth, very little is known about what the Celestial Council is. People, who are even slightly aware, can't be sure of their thoughts on the subject. While the mystery of the Council's very existence is intentional design, it is possible for those of flesh to find ways of making contact with spiritual governance.

Over a hundred miles away from Station-7, Maya drives down a mostly secluded state highway cut into the mountain foothills as directed in the escape plan. Her next goal is to reach a remote gas station near the end of the foothills by about four o'clock that afternoon. White noise is broadcasting from the radio and mixing with the sound of wind in open windows.

Driving provided an opportunity to review events over the past two days in detail and attempt to process them. Certain parts made a lot of sense while others were difficult to stomach.

The whole concept her father discovered an answer to chaotic theory for example, this is an incredible feat, and nearly too good to be true. Maya understood her father to be very intelligent, secretive, and truthful. She could not find a reason to doubt his claim, it was futile to try.

In fact, every attempt to refute the notion eventually turned into optimistic thoughts of what someone could do with this kind of knowledge. A major realization for Maya is an understanding of how traditional monetary systems would succumb to chaotic prediction and crumble in their place.

A solution to randomness means a lot of things, but mostly how the world would be very different from what it is now. Maya thought of a few terrifying ways one answer to chaotic theory could revolutionize the planet.

At the top level, if attained by the masses, the globe spins into a boring place where surprises no longer exist. Anything and everything are known beforehand when randomness ceases. Though, an important question is how would this algorithm predict human spontaneity? Is it able to accurately reveal future thought patterns?

If only a select few could leverage such an ability, the outcome is likely very different, and closely guided by personal moral philosophies. By nature, people have proven throughout history, too much power corrupts ethics and establishes dire situations for those without it.

One example is, imagine having the ability to precisely predict financial markets while the majority of investors rely on company reports and statistical data. Furthermore, there is a possibility to stay undetected if the ability is applied in an intelligent way.

In the wrong hands, morally, a solution to everything random places an individual beyond all institutions, beyond federal reserves, and beyond central banks. Applying the theory to markets has the capability of essentially bankrupting the world.

Computers with programs using random number generation are susceptible to what Maya considers, an anti-algorithm, or the chaos formula. With it, prediction breaks heuristic constraint and foretelling the future is not fantasy.

We become binary, in a sense, by knowing or not knowing; Maya sees one of many possible outcomes with more emphasis than others. This very vision places mankind in a position capable of transcending physics in its present form.

"Funny," she thought out loud. "All of these brilliant scientific minds searching for anti-matter, anti-particles, and anti-gravity. What about anti-algorithms? The master anti-formula; a force able to undo everything people have created to explain scientific reality."

Maya's deep thoughts are put on hold when an old weather-beaten wooden road sign passes by stating the town of Silverville is ten miles ahead. The rendezvous point is Westgate's Garage, a small service station stuck in the boonies, and the only place to fill-up for miles.

Silverville is a curious ghost town remnant of a booming gold rush from decades past. In fact, this town's name refers to a silver deposit found about a mile west. Prospectors discovered a little gold and a whole lot of silver at the time. A small mining operation built a few shelters and a weigh station with hopes of hitting a lode, but the mines dried up and the prospectors left town.

Westgate's Garage is conveniently located at a crossroads connecting the foothills highway, orientated in the general direction of east to west, to a north-south supply route highway.

Rundown buildings on either side of the 70's service station is effective at repelling most travelers passing through. The only residents are Bill Westgate and his black lab, Shadow, who enjoy passing time together on the porch; overlooking the pumps and a distant horizon.

Shadow rests on the deck, beside an empty chair, with her eyes closed and legs stretched out to the toes for comfort. The sound of a vehicle causes calculated ear twitches, placing the location of the car, but this reaction is no more dramatic than a light twitch casting a fly off her fur. Bill, who would normally occupy the chair, was absent from view.

Maya slowly rolls into one of the garage bays and leaves the vehicle with her tactical bag. She walks around to the back of the car and jumps to grab a rope for closing the door. Shutting the garage darkened everything, making it difficult to see for a moment, but the flick of a switch lit a small service light overhead.

She was slightly nervous inside the garage after reading some of Jack's cautionary notes from earlier that day. He mentioned how Bill isn't who he seemed to be, but to not lead on like she knows if there happens to be a confrontation. The plan involves having Bill think everything is normal, everyday business.

To help calm her nerves a little, Maya went into the garage restroom for a moment to splash some water on her face, and then take a bathroom break. She pulled herself together, deciding to not spend any more time than necessary, and left the garage through a side exit.

A security camera outside, above the side door, watched as Maya walked down the highway heading south. Bill was inside the attached house, viewing the camera on a small monitor. He picked up a cell phone and made a call after seeing which direction Maya went.

"Southbound it is," Bill said firmly with a straight lip, and then hung up the phone.

Dusk descended on the town of Silverville as Maya walked down the highway shoulder. The car she dropped off at Westgate's will be chopped, parted out, and boxed in crates for later shipment. Bill is a longtime friend of the family who has a knack with these types of tasks; he was prompted ahead of time by Jack to arrange the drop off.

Jack and Bill grew up together and they would really do anything for each other. When the Westgate's were facing difficult times financially, Jack bought the town land at a state auction, for a surprisingly low figure, and gifted the deed to Bill. This helped save the service station but it did not stop Bill's wife, Bridget, from leaving him for life in the city.

The highway became darker, followed by cold rain, and Maya's cadence with her thoughts remained as consistent as the steps she takes. Now she feels like a wandering nomad more than ever before; and rather enjoys it by a smile on her face despite the chill.

Instead of fearing isolation and the lack of a permanent home, she is thrilled to embrace the unknown. For Maya, there is no matter of sacrifice too great to fetter her determination.

Just then, she noticed the highway ahead gradually light up from semi-truck headlights. She turned around and walked backwards while gazing at the truck as rain skirted across the beams on an angle. The vehicle began slowing down, and with the sound of air escaping the brakes, the truck halted next to her. It was difficult to see past tinted windows and a little caution seemed necessary at the time. The passenger side automatic window then rolled down.

"You look a little wet there," Said the driver in a gentle voice.

Maya was dripping water and very eager to ward off the dampness. "Yes, I was really hoping it would miss us." She replied with an eye-roll.

The driver thought she might be defensive but elected to tell her anyway, "I can bring you as far as the next town, if you like."

He clears his throat and continues, "I'll be on this road tonight until reaching Moonvale," with a look of seriousness.

Dusty appeared to be in a permanent state of limbo between wide-awake and over-tired. He is a little rough around the edges, but otherwise very healthy for spending long hours on the road. Dusty utilizes time off the clock exercising in attempt to counteract sitting for most of the day.

Maya thought to herself, darting her eyes upward, and decided she could handle this risk if need be. "You're a life-saver, thank you." She said.

After pulling the door open, Maya jumped up to the passenger seat and leaned out the door slightly to wring water out of her hair. She then nestled her tactical bag on the floor between her feet and fastened her seatbelt.

"My name is Dusty Thomas; it's a pleasure to meet you." The driver said.

Maya, surprised at his manners and candid disposition, realized she wouldn't have to worry as much. "Dusty, well thanks again for the lift. My name is Erin." she replied using the first name that popped into her head.

Dusty was excited to have company for the first time in a long time. He started getting chatty as he let off the brakes and geared up to speed.

"Oh, it's no problem at all really. I figure as much, we're both going in the same direction you know. I had an empty seat over there and nobody real to talk with. Also, I enjoy helping those who sincerely need it. Anyone walking this highway at night in the cold rain could use a little help."

If true, this provided Maya with further peace of mind, but she still remained reluctant to let her guard down any more than it already is.

The two clicked and conversed for a while driving this lonely highway. Certain qualities in Dusty reminded Maya of her father, such as caring for others while maintaining your own, something which sincerely showed over time.

Short bouts of expected awkward silence broke some conversations apart, but there were several periods of comfortable silence, between two people who suddenly found they have similar core values.

The chatter eased up a bit as Maya settled in for the long haul. Dusty tried to give her space for processing between thoughts, and she had a flashback during one of those times.

***

A gentle breeze whirled through Maya's dark hair as she sat with her legs crossed in an open meadow not far from the family farm. Her bangs fluttered as they graced her forehead and cheeks.

The sun shimmered in her deep green eyes as moonlight reflects in the snow. This memory from her early twenties is one Maya would often revisit as a defining time in her life. It was shortly after her mom passed away, she found refuge in the meadow as a reminder of peace and serenity of her mother, Julia.

In memory of the loss, Maya performed a ritual intended to connect to the spirit world of the universe. First, she tied her hair back in a ponytail, allowing her neck feel the breeze. Then, she took a smudge stick from her pack, cupped one hand over it, and kept a flame lit on the end until smoke surged upward. She mustered courage to fight angst and quietly spoke, with trembling lips, as small tears rolled down the side of her face.

"Spirits of the land let this sage billow into the wind as an offering of peace. Mom, please forgive me and let the spirits of the north, south, east, and west watch over you. Let the smell of sage forgive all creatures of the land touched by its wind, for it is neither my deed nor my will to be part of acts which curse those the wind touches directly or indirectly."

Maya stood up from the grass while slowly waving sage smoke across wildflower tops. The air whipped around in a sudden gust causing a series of eddies to form.

A small stream of smoke swirls upward, blankets across her face, and she closes her eyes. Seconds later she opens her eyelids to reveal an ethereal green glow slip over the pupils. She took a light breath in with a fading exhale and continued with the ritual.

"Desire for control places people in bearish conflict with the natural order of things. Acts of ignorance place savages among innocents, bawdry among continence, and beasts among flowers loathing even their own blood enough to remove it from the living; and those who leave it dangling in blatant disregard as a tool for vile perpetuation."

Her words were not loud, but they echoed and reverberated around her very being. At this moment, Maya found herself deeply entwined with everything, and with her soul vulnerably exposed.

Swirling sage smoke encircled with more ferocity than before, this time collecting flower petals and meadow grass, forming itself into a human shape. A face Maya recognized protruded from the swirling debris and spoke calmly with certitude.

"Spirits of the north, south, east and west, hear your voice and smell sweet sage, Maya. I am known as Cassandra, whom souls and flesh doubt my words, cursed to speak in cosmic tongues for all of eternity as a walker of dreams. I too, witness pestilence rampant across lands of this planet, and the soil too, is parted and divisively portioned for it to be undying in the vice of life's ravagers."

***

Suddenly she begins to faintly hear a rough manly voice displacing Cassandra. "Hey, are you alright there; daydreaming?" Dusty asked Maya after noticing she was staring blankly out the front window.

"Oh hey, yes. I'm good, just recollecting old memories is all. The field over there reminds me of a time long ago when I discovered more about my beliefs." She points to the left at a swath of rolling prairie grass only partially visible in the truck's headlights and moonlight.

Dusty looked over at Maya and questioned her, "Do you know what I believe?"

She blinks and presses her lips together while thinking if she really wants to disrupt the reminiscing.

"I can see you're not sure, but I'm going to tell you anyway. It's not often I have the pleasure of company." He continued eerily, almost as if he could see directly into Maya's past right then.

"They call death eternal sleep for a reason. Every night, people think they fall asleep, when they're actually dying. They just wake up the next day and pick up where their life left off. Death is just like any other night except we don't wake up the next day."

"Now that's an interesting way of looking at life." Maya responded. She then felt like exploring his theory further and asked, "Where do you think we go then, during the eternal sleep? Do we keep dreaming and those dreams become a new reality for us then?"

Dusty appeared flustered and said, "You know, I didn't really think that far past not waking up again."

Maya raised left eyebrow, wondering how Dusty thought that deeply about life and didn't seem the least bit curious to know what happens in the end besides sleeping. "If death is a slumber, then what do you believe happens in our dreams?" Maya responded.

Dusty wanted to continue without really acknowledging her question. He said, "Well, take me for example. I drive this truck, every day, and I don't think too much about it. I go home and die, wake up the next day, and drive this truck again. I don't talk a lot, but once in a while someone like you needs a lift. There's a little interaction and my day goes on to die again and repeat."

Maya is a little worried now. "That sounds a little depressing," she responded while thinking, there's always a risk to hitchhiking, she knows this, and this driver could be an unhinged one.

Dusty continued rambling, "Every day I think to myself. What would happen if one day, as I drove my route, and just grabbed the wheel out of nowhere, while cruising at 70 mph, and cranked a hard right. I bet the trailer would whip around and the truck would roll. Then, the next day, I would just wake up again to drive the same route."

The look of fear and shock on Maya's face was not easily hidden from Dusty. Having just met him, she didn't know if he was messing around or truly losing it. "You know," she said, "some people might consider that a little suicidal, but I too have wondered what the universe would think if I just suddenly did something it didn't expect me to do. What would happen then?"

Dusty starts laughing, almost maniacally. "I know! That's exactly what I mean." He said. "It's a thrilling thought! I honestly don't have interest in finding out. I mean, I don't want to hurt anyone because of something I did, you know?"

Maya felt a sense of relief now and happily responded with a little flattery to curb his deviance further. "Dusty, you're an alright guy, you know."

By this time Maya was close enough to her destination, as she felt comfortable with anyway, and asked Dusty to pull over. She opens the door, slides off the seat and steps out.

Dusty says, "Hey wait, Erin, you didn't tell me what you believe happens when we die. What do you think happens when we die?"

She glances down the road, with her hand on the door, and states with strong conviction, "I think we turn into balls of light and disappear into thin air."

You could see the wheels turning with a subtle look of confusion on Dusty's face. "Balls of light you say? I hope you get to where you're going before that can happen!" He said with an awkward smile.

"You too, it was good chatting with you. Keep on hauling and thanks for the lift!" Maya added, and then shut the door. She lightly slapped the door twice, letting Dusty know it's closed, and he drove off.

***

Bill is a tall, lanky middle-aged fellow who prefers a solitary lifestyle by limiting interaction with big cities. He is known for testing society, often without discernible reason, from a distance. Country life is his forte and strangers who meet him for the first time usually have a strangely odd and unexplainable feeling over the encounter.

He is an inquisitive person with a penchant for cleanliness and order, yet spends most days in overalls covered in dirt and grime. It's necessary for Bill to keep his mind busy; otherwise he tends to wander off mid-thought, thinking about the life he once aspired to live.

His father, John, worked for a clandestine military operation for twenty years until reported missing in action. As a child, Bill dreamed of being just like his father and often spent time alone, pretending to be on his own secret missions. From what Bill can remember, his father rarely visited, and this fueled imagination to great lengths.

After high school, Bill joined the military with hopes of moving up the ranks into a secret ops position, but this did not pan out as intended right away. The military honorably discharged him under high year tenure after completing one term of service without selection for promotion.

It devastated him.

Nevertheless, he wanted the family to be proud, even without a military career, and decided to help his mother running Westgate's Garage in Silverville. Bill and his wife moved in next door, occupying an old six-bedroom motel left behind from the mining boom.

Although the garage wasn't exactly what Bill wanted with his life, he found ways to make it fun and profitable for the family. One instance was to increase traffic through town, which lacked by only serving an east to west route. He petitioned the state to reposition a proposed north-south route through it as well.

Locating the new road a few miles west of original plans ultimately saves the state thousands in construction. The state planning office didn't see the savings until Bill's letter spelled it out, and they were quick to agree with his findings.

The new highway bisecting Silverville brought additional revenue, though not enough to live as comfortably as Bill's wife Bridget desired.

Chapter 4

Lost Soul

Bridget became tired of living in a remote town with barely any interaction with people other than the Westgate's. The garage didn't interest her much and neither did helping with Bill's mother, Edna. Over time, Bridget's true self began to show which contradicted Bill often and frequently.

Bill's attention however, focused primarily on his mother who fell progressively ill from slow-onset brain cancer. Eventually, the only help was for him to be there and comfort Edna. He tried to coax Bridget into doing more in this time of need, but only managed to push her further away. Bill knew things were about to change and did his best to stay diligent.

Months after Edna's passing, Bridget feels more alone than ever before. She may have not helped comfort Edna, or Bill for that matter, but it's having people around that helped Bridget cope with her situation. When Edna passed away, the focus snapped back to the now distant relationship with Bill; until one day Bridget decided it was time to move on.

Determined to move on as well, after losing his mother and wife, Bill traveled to the next town called Moonvale in search of company. He went to the animal shelter and adopted a black lab puppy, naming her Shadow, as the absence of light in his life. Later he would realize Shadow became the light of his life as his best friend.

Business from fuel fill-ups, flat repairs and occasional overheated engines slowed up enough that Bill started looking for other opportunities. With some money in savings, he covertly built an underground chop shop operation. One garage bay lift was modified to lower vehicles into a basement workshop while appearing and functioning as a standard vehicle lift. In this area, he could easily hide a vehicle from the outside world.

The pay was considerable enough that he could now get through several months from one client alone. Surprisingly, he did not have to look hard for clients either. One in particular would show up almost regularly after a job removing the identification number stamped into the car frame.

This, at least, is most of what Jack knew about Bill since the honorable discharge. A good portion of Bill's life had been intentionally left out to protect his true identity. As careful as Jack had been about nearly everything, he managed to stay one step ahead of Bill at the same time.

The first clues for Jack came from Bill's relationship with Bridget. She attempted to warn Jack several times during visits, until blatantly telling him, "Be careful about Billy, he is not the same man you knew years ago, do some digging; and take this." She handed Jack a small black silk bag with items she collected. It is apparent Bridget left Bill under very different circumstances.

"He's not hitting you, is he?" Jack asked firmly with concern.

Bridget replied without hesitation, "No, no, it's not like that, Bill may be aggressive but he wouldn't hurt me. Please, just check the bag later. I have to go."

Taking the potential threat seriously, how Bill may not be who he seems to be, Jack hacked into a government computer to find out more about Mr. Westgate. While the bag contents might be helpful, Jack needed to put what Bridget said into context before continuing.

Jack slipped into the Moonvale military recruiting office and took over the open machine, then manipulated the access. Personnel records were located through exploiting a loophole the military cyber command didn't know about at the time. Conveniently for Jack, a recruiting officer forgot to lock a terminal during lunchtime which made things a lot easier.

The recruiting office isn't a very busy one, but it does attract enough applicants to stay open. It's a bland office with a brown theme, posters on the walls, and a wooden stand full of career choice pamphlets. Though the office is unappealing and outdated, military policy states the use of flashy marketing gimmicks and ploys to get recruits is detraction from a true reality of service.

On most days, a single officer watches over things and has to find ways to stay occupied when bored. Lately the officer on duty has obsessed over a pocket television to watch sports and game shows with the volume cranked up; in what might also be considered detraction from good standard of service.

Bill's record indicates he went from basic training to a position in Geolocation Operations after completion, on referral from John Westgate, his father. The record is clean over thirty years and wraps up neatly with active duty retirement. His pension amount is hidden, the same with his last known location and a portion of the current security clearance line, all marred by black lines.

The file hints that a high-ranking official in the forces cleaned up Bill's record. Jack knows a shiny service history with multiple redactions, on active duty retirement, means the active duty part is an open door to secret ops recruitment.

Suspicions of Bill's activity are somewhat validated by his military file, but there is no way they would blatantly expose him to anyone with basic access to the system. With new details, Jack backed out of the personnel profile screen to hide his presence, but he typed too fast and backed all the way to a login screen.

He left the recruiting office, walked a block down the street and hopped into an inconspicuous dark green sedan. It was a humid day with very little breeze to alleviate the inflated temperature, yet Jack rolled down the windows for airflow instead of turning on the engine for cooling.

The recruitment officer left the bathroom and went back to his desk. He remained fixated on the pocket television and cursed at people playing game shows, "There's no way that range set is five grand, bid a dollar, moron!"

"Hey, this thing is asking for a username and password?" He questioned after glancing over at the computer screen.

"Ah well, I guess it does that sometimes," the officer said before logging back in.

Meanwhile, down the street in the car, Jack inspected the pouch Bridget gave him to look for more clues about Bill's double-life; there is a point when Bridget noticed Bill acting differently from normal, in a scary kind of way, and it prompted her to keep details. The small silk bag happened to be from one of her perfume bottles and the thin fabric made it easy for her to conceal inside her bra or purse.

He dumped the bag out and found a stubby key stamped with a number on one side and the word "Highrock" on the reverse. Other contents included a mini cassette tape, small pad of paper, and a photograph of Bill with an unknown, yet familiar looking woman.

The papers contained a log of when Bill left Silverville without letting Bridget know. On those days, he seemed distracted prior to disappearing, and he didn't want to talk much about things after returning. Often, he would say something generally related to Highrock, but that's the most detail she could get without sounding too suspicious.

At first, Jack didn't recognize the woman standing with Bill in the photograph. They looked happy together, dressed in formal attire, walking out of Last Amigo Saloon in Moonvale; a candid moment with every indication the couple did not know they were being watched. Jack smiled, thinking about how Bridget went to great lengths to find out what Bill was up to.

Then he notices a subtle detail in the photograph she may have missed, a tiny wire loop slightly exposed above Bill's collar. It must have bunched up at some point during dinner. Looking at the wire direction allowed Jack to locate a small camera embedded in a tie clip. Jack then assumed the woman was Bill's mark, but couldn't make sense of why.

Another look at the photograph jogged his memory and Jack is able to identify the woman as Tina Reedman. It didn't make sense to Jack, why Bill would be recording her, because she is known for being a sweet and kind person.

As far as Jack knows, Tina works for the Highrock Chamber helping local businesses with job placement opportunities for young adults. It would be out of character to have her surveilled, though perhaps the Chamber is a cover and she has a dark side he is unaware of.

At the post office in Highrock, Jack walks down a narrow corridor of mailboxes, scanning box numbers for one matching the purse key. The silk bag didn't contain any notes about the key and checking out the post office is a guess at this stage.

The post box numbers didn't line up and the sequence seemed off. Jack took a moment to sit on a small bench located under a tinted window at the end of the corridor. He looked at the key in his hand, moving it to reflect the overhead light, and flipped around a few times.

Jack notices a company name inscribed on the backside of the key in a tiny font. At first, he thought it referred to a key company, who possibly made a duplicate, but then presumed it could be for a storage unit.

This idea occurred to him after noticing a flier for storage units, tucked into a bundle of newspapers, sitting on the floor next to the bench. He pulled the flier from under a yellow banding strap. The paper ad confirmed the key belongs to a storage unit by a matching company name in small print at the bottom of the flier.

"I was thinking too small," said Jack with a light chuckle.

He left the post office, stopped for a quick bite, and then went over to check out the storage flier lead. During the drive, Jack thought about what Bill would need an entire storage unit for. This could be a lot bigger discovery than he first imagined, or it could be nothing at all.

There's also a possibility Bill knew Bridget was steadily gaining insight and he moved the incriminating evidence well before others could find it. On top of this, Jack also acknowledged the fact this could be an orchestrated trap. However, he trusted Bridget by her disposition, and had trouble finding reasons to doubt it.

He opened the storage unit, yanked a pull chain light, and shut the door just enough to allow a little air in.

The storage area was mostly empty with the exception of seven banker's boxes stacked off to the side, a table, and a chair. One of the boxes had its lid removed and placed upside down on an adjacent box. Hanging file folders filled the open box with a gap between a few, which either looked like a folder had been pulled or the others were pushed aside to put a file back.

"Going with low tech, I see," stated Jack.

The folders are numbered, followed by a family name with no first or middle name initials. He scanned across the files, pushing each one behind the last, until one in particular caught his attention; Kaona Family.

Now visibly disturbed by the folder he just picked up, Jack questioned in frustration, "What would he be doing with this one? Kaona is hardly a common name around here."

The folder contained hand typed profiles of Jack and his family. Each page contained a brief biography, contact detail, last known whereabouts, and a photo stapled to the side. Why there's a case file on the Kaona's is beyond Jack at this point.

He searched through other files, trying to find a common element which might provide a clue to the cache. There are many commonalities, every folder contained profile information about people in the community, laid out in the format.

He opened another box, and then another, and found the same types of files.

There must have been a few hundred files here at least, possibly the entire town, he thought. Jack tried to make sense of the stash, and why Bill stored so many profiles, but now at least knew the apparent truth from Bill about Westgate's Garage was fabrication.

Though it seemed odd at first, one box was filled with many sheets of jet-black paper. A closer inspection revealed the sheets were actually photo paper overexposed to light. He pulled a piece out and tucked it away in an inside jacket pocket for later inspection.

Beside the stack of files is a cheap chair and round card table. An antique typewriter and ash tray are on the table closest to the chair. A couple replacement typewriter ribbons and an open ream of paper appear to be shoved off to the side. An LED backlit analog clock with a stuck second-hand ticks on the tin wall directly opposite of the chair.

Searching the table reveals a curious clue. A sheet of paper fed into the typewriter reads, "In a realm where shadow meets light?" This happens to indicate that Bill, or whoever typed it, knew a founding principal of Jack's research. In the anti-algorithm concept, the event horizon as it were, is the fine line separating existence from inexistence.

Just then, the typewriter shook with a ding noise, and the paper fed itself to a new line. The words, "Time is the only waste of time," punched out letter by letter.

A whooshing noise from the wall behind the table started randomly. Jack snapped his head upward and looked at the clock. The face spun frantically in place while the hour, minute, and second hands remained frozen at seven o'clock.

The clock spinning is a little much Jack to process and he almost felt ill from watching reality bend before his eyes as he stumbled to the door, visibly shaken from the experience. He couldn't explain the event scientifically and that scared him enough to stir a bit of panic.

He left the storage facility to follow up on a final lead from Bridget by heading over to the Highrock shopping center for a micro cassette player. While sitting in the store parking lot, he removed packaging from a new player and slid the purse tape in for a listen.

"No, no, I'm positive he doesn't know we're watching," Claimed a voice resembling Bill on the tape. "Everything is advancing; I'll send over some details."

An unknown male voice then replied, "We need to find out. Whatever this is, he's creating ripples in time. We need to get our hands on this, and him taken care of, pronto."

By now, Jack couldn't decide which was worse, irrefutable confirmation of Bill's deception and detail of an undercover investigation, or the crazy clock and typewriter experience from earlier at the storage unit moments ago. Jack's best guess about the tape comments relate to work on an anti-algorithm formula and several hushed chaos experiments.

The fringe tests were mostly secretive with the exception of obtaining supplies here and there. Results were kept confidential, meaning really that only he knew, but what the tests disrupted could have been noticed. In fact, he didn't really have a solid method at the time of understanding the scope of fallout.

He imagined the experiments affected the world much like constant string theorem. Change in his immediate vicinity yanked virtual strings attached to mass somewhere else on the planet. What exactly was affected at the time is difficult to determine, but this suggests something happened.

A female voice on the tape, "I have a tail on the wife and daughter. They appear completely dark about Jack. Do I continue or is there another task?"

The tape played static for five seconds and an unknown male voice replied, "Maybe try to get a little closer, and if things get gnarly, you know what to do."

Jack became angry hearing those words. It meant only one thing to him, that his wife Julia became an unintended casualty for the work he is involved in. The voices on the tape, and possibly Bill, seemed to be after Jack's knowledge. When progress toward uncovering the truth became too difficult, they sent someone after his family.

For two years, Jack believed he lost his wife to a mysteriously strange accident, and the new findings are reason enough to believe the woman on the tape was responsible. It also occurred to Jack, the fact Bridget knew about this well before anything happened to Julia.

To keep straight with Bill, while remaining undetected, Jack elected not to confront him with evidence. The strategy became an honest effort to essentially play into Bill's hands, when possible without raising suspicion, like the revelation never happened. Later on, this would prove effective in the master anti-algorithm plan.

The idea became especially difficult as Jack spiraled in thought about what possibly happened to his wife. Analyzing the blackened photo paper exacerbated mournful dread because it reminded him of the storage locker and case files.

"She was a deeply caring person and didn't deserve this to happen to her." He claimed while trying to hold back his emotions.

Subtle wrinkles on his forehead protruded even more as he raised his eyebrows up. A sick feeling washed over his face as he stammered, "It's my entire fault. This wouldn't have happened if I just left well enough alone."

Jack grasped at the wheel with both hands, at ten and two, and bowed forward into the horn area; saying once more, "My entire fault."

Chapter 5

Countdown

Maya covered a fair bit of ground in the dark after Dusty dropped her off. She needed to be extra careful, even though he seemed like a nice guy, and not give too much detail to anyone. This is the same reason why she asked him to pull over about an hour's walk from her destination.

On the walk, Maya once again reviewed her father's plan and all of the chaos quickly unfolding over the past two days. She found it odd that Bill wasn't around when dropping the car off, but was glad to dodge confrontation. It was also strange to her, how Shadow didn't budge when she drove up to the bay door.

For this leg of the journey, Maya needs to locate Muddy Creek bisecting a bend in the road, and follow the southern riverbank to a crossing. It's the preferred route due to ruggedness on the north bank.

This river itself is not very large, at ten feet wide and a foot deep on average, but is still a vital source of mountain runoff to the nearby area that can get a tad swift under the right conditions.

Muddy Creek runs roughly west to east and has flat farmland for miles to the south, while the north side features a privately owned, forest area slowly encroaching across the creek. Hundreds of years ago, during the prospecting days, this river served as a gold panning destination. However, the gold dried up and left prospectors with mud; naming the creek as such in spite.

The manmade rock bridge is designed to blend in with large and small rocks scattered in the area, and serves three important purposes.

One, it provides a somewhat dry way to cross the creek. Two, the elevated stones force water to rush over them like rapids, which can be heard from some distance. The third is simply for a quaint countryside aesthetic appeal next to miles of farmland, though some would say, not as quaint as a curved wooden bridge would do, but far less conspicuous, considering.

Maya hopped over the creek and into dense brush on the other side. A narrow pathway, nearly overgrown, directs her deeper into the thicket. The moon is now at its maximum height in the sky and illuminates everything around her like a feathery white veil slowly floating to the ground. Tall grass and tree leaves were motionless in the air. She could only hear her footsteps and thighs breaking foliage as she pushed further.

Using the same technique as the mountain cavern path, Maya pulled out her black light torch and made steady sweeps ahead of her. This time she locates an emblem at eye-level on a tree and pulls down on a stubby branch protruding from the trunk. The stub activates a trapdoor next to the tree which slides open to reveal a set of stone steps leading downward.

Once inside the crypt, Maya yanks on a dim wall sconce to close the trapdoor above her. The room here is a narrow L-shaped hallway with an iron gate at the end. A dirt bike, supported by its kickstand, is off to the side and covered in moss with a helmet hanging off the outside handle grip.

Roots are scattered across the ceiling and partially down stone slab walls. Moisture trickles through the cracks, dripping between ledges, and echoes lightly in the hallway as droplets patter off the stone. Again, like the mountain cavern, she presses on a biometric sensor to open the gate and proceeds into Station-6 with celerity.

The footprint of this station isn't quite as large as the last, with only two rooms, but it's still packed with technology and basic amenities. Maya went into the power room, containing a battery array connected to a hydrothermal turbine in the creek, and checked the levels. After that, she used the vault toilet in the corner of the room; she just couldn't hold it any longer.

Maya then went to the other room and sat on a wooden crate next to a handmade table. A laptop with a black screen idles while waiting for input. Maya taps a key, the screen lights up, and prompts for authentication. Placing the first USB dongle from Station-7 starts a confirmation which she then finishes by pressing her thumb to a biometric sensor on the dongle.

Status details of the station pop-up, along with a warning note claiming Station-7 is down. This confirms, beyond a smoke plume, the prior exit sequence effectively disabled those systems. Beside the status window is a set of instructions on the screen, similar to notes from the last station.

The exit strategy here is different in terms of execution, yet it still requires Maya to be rested. She locks the computer, a force of habit really, and heads over to a portable cot near the table. Taking a load off, Maya sits on the canvas and stretches her feet over the side. It's been a few long days in a row and she wondered if these clues will continue on as they have been.

She takes her shoes off, rubs her feet for a moment, and then pivots around to rest. A single pillow supports her head, but the thin blankets are not very helpful in the way of comfort on canvas. Even though she didn't read the notes thoroughly, she did catch a line about heading to Turkey next.

In a way, Maya felt some comfort knowing transit would allow for more time to relax on the way, and she drifts off to sleep.

Several hours later, small water drops start falling from the ceiling to her feet. The droplets seemed to have no effect for a while, but soon they manage waking her. She kicked at the air, let out a sigh of frustration, and retracted her feet away from the end of the cot. Now that Maya is awake, she decides to get up and review the day's plan.

After changing socks with a dry pair from her tactical bag, Maya wakes up the laptop. A set of instructions on the screen detail how to retrieve the next segment of the anti-algorithm and an exit plan. This one isn't quite as involved as the last, but requires timing on her part.

First, she executes a script on the computer which gives fifteen minutes from trigger to reach a safe distance. She pushes a blasting cap into a hole in the ceiling above the laptop, then heads over to the power room and plugs three blasting caps into compound pasted to the wall behind the battery array, and a final cap into a battery midway up the rack.

The laptop recognizes all blasting caps are attached and remote starts the dirt bike. Two LCD screens above the handlebars light up; one screen is a digital speedometer with mileage counter, and the other with a fifteen-minute countdown timer. The headlight turns on and shines a beam through its moss covering toward the stairs as the engine starts gurgling.

A metal tray attached to the underside of the computer depressurizes and lets out a hissing sound followed by a mechanical squeak. The tray ejects with a payload of Maya's next action items, including segment number two of the secretive anti-algorithm on a secondary USB stick. As soon as she picks up the payload, a pressure sensor will start the detonation timer.

Before grabbing the items, Maya spends a moment to take a deep breath, knowing the next move is particularly dangerous if for some reason there are any faults in the system or wiring. She feels more comfortable with an active trigger that she controls, but this passive mechanism presents a potential problem; if it doesn't fire off, she can't afford to double-back into a disastrous situation.

She must trust the system her father built, and the instructions, if she's going to make it to the next location. Taking the extra time to cover tracks is a necessary part of her father's plan based on the magnitude of knowledge at stake.

One positive thought here is, once Maya grabs the payload, she will have the majority of anti-algorithm code, plus directions to Station-5 and the Kayseri fragment. Everything should work out provided she reaches her destination quickly, even with a detonation issue.

Maya opens a camera monitor window on the laptop and uses the keyboard controls to pan around outside. The camera is embedded into a tree branch, and camouflaged, above the hatch to provide an undetected view of the surroundings. Everything looks good to her; with no movement in the brush or in the field across the creek.

She snags the payload, a pressure sensor alerts the program, and the self-destruct sequence initiates; this sequence also forces the stairway hatch to automatically open. Maya dips a shoulder into a tactical strap and flips her bag to her back. She places the payload in a zipped pocket inside her jacket, zips up, and heads to the dirt bike.

Maya takes the helmet off the outer handle grip and puts it on. A wireless sensor inside the helmet recognizes her action and lights up a data display overlaying the visor glass. Data populating on the visor is aggregated from a series of sensors planted in the bike and the feedback looks like it's projected ahead of her for a more comfortable feel.

A horizontal green line, with a centralized targeting box, tracks the changing terrain using elevation hash markers. Various machine health metrics including speed, fuel supply, compass, and engine temperature display on the bottom left. Mileage, atomic time, and countdown time metrics are displayed on the bottom right; clearly, the handlebar gauges are for helmet back-up.

Environment feedback is especially helpful for Maya, considering she only has less than three hours of lifetime dirt bike experience and already feels nervous about having to ride. She hops on, knocks the kickstand, and rocks the throttle. The engine reverberates throughout as its exhaust forces air outward. Maya pulls the clutch, kick-shifts the bike into gear, and propels ahead up the stairs.

Thick brush outside of the bunker whips across the dirt bike and Maya's legs as she forces her way through. She reaches the creek and skips across the stone path while splashing cold water everywhere. Now on the other side of the creek, water runs down the fenders and cakes with field dirt, flinging wildly into the air; all systems look nominal on the heads-up visor screen.

With the countdown clock showing nine minutes remaining, an automatic mechanism closes the bunker hatch, and Maya proceeds to lean back to relax. Her destination is an airport in the city of Lexton, which is roughly two-hundred miles southeast from point A to B, and she's crossing farm fields to get there. Keeping away from roadways minimizes the number of people who might see her. It also gives her a chance to think and enjoy the ride.

As she cruises along the field, Maya gazes at the horizon and thinks, "the world is a beautiful place. There's a blue sky with puffy clouds in the distance and trees dotting the horizon in their own quaint way. The visual blur from a flow of a field rushing past a dirt bike at 60mph," Then she is interrupted by a blipping ping noise like an old radar unit, and a blinking countdown timer in the visor.

Maya keeps an eye on the rear-view mirror with ten seconds left in the exit sequence. The visor and handlebar countdown both report a success, but the signs of bunker implosion are hardly visible in a shaking mirror from this distance. A status signal in the visor reports a Station-6 connection loss. It appears everything went as planned again and Maya pushes forward.

Something strange happened at the bunker right after the explosion though. A set of vines crawl through the grass and lash around the trap door, which is now dented upward from the blast. The vines snake around, coiling into springs, and form thick vegetation to obscure the door from view.

Thought process continues as Maya begins contemplating the deeper side of her actions. "As beautiful as a natural world can be, humans still manage to leave chaos in the wake of action, and shadows lurk where light may have once reached. Yet, in some respects, this is a natural event itself, like a volcano or earthquake."

Nearly halfway on the journey to Lexton and Maya is feeling the effects of long-haul riding.

The fuel supply switched to reserve not long ago, which gave a few extra miles, but she will have to stop soon to fill up and take a breather. A grassy mound up ahead, oddly betwixt rows of dirt, looks inviting for a picnic.

The knoll resembles an old burial mound, covered in terse verdure, contrasting the barren landscape. Tracks show a conscientious effort to neatly plow around the hill instead of gradually forcing it into oblivion. Perhaps it's a special place to the farmer, or a demonstration of respect for the environment, but surely well-kept either way.

In observation of the mound, Maya elects to park in a dirt trough beside the hill. She puts the kickstand down, gets off the bike, and places her helmet on the seat. While walking around in a small circle, stretching aching muscles, Maya takes in a gentle breeze and bright blue skies she considered as beautiful earlier on.

Maya detaches a canister from the bike's rear rack and proceeds to refuel. This should be enough to reach Lexton from here, but there is another small emergency cylinder on the rack if needed. After refueling the bike, Maya wipes her hands on a rag and then decides to sit down at the base of the grassy hill for a nutrition bar.

She can lean back from here to look at the sky, or close her eyes and listen to nature, both as good relief from recent chaos for no shadows cast on the face of the hill. Temporarily anyway, Maya feels the knoll is a harmonized place, as clouds are gathering. She should stay ahead of the incoming weather and prepares to continue the trek.

Without spending too much time relaxing on the grass, basking in the sun, Maya returned to the dirt bike and put the helmet back on. Once again, she drove off toward the horizon with haste. The weather brewing behind her is gradually looking more ominous as the sun disappears and sky darkens.

When a few rain drops hit the visor and jacket, Maya realizes she won't be able to out-pace the gusty storm rolling in. She can see the Lexton skyline coming into focus. Maya scans around for an abandoned farm, as mentioned in the Station-6 notes to be somewhere on the edge of Lexton city limits.

Meanwhile, in Silverville, Dusty pulls up to the pumps. He shuts the engine off and gets out of the truck to start the fill up, then walks over to talk to Bill. As he strolls over to the porch, he perks up and says, "Hey there!"

With a smile, Bill questions, "Hello Dusty. How goes the battle? I see weather over there, but it looks like a miss here."

Dusty replies, "Yep! I really can't complain at that, it's heading south."

As one of the few regulars to Westgate's Garage, Dusty has built a rapport with Bill over the years. The conversations usually didn't progress beyond small talk. This is partially because Dusty regularly sensed paranoia from Bill and didn't want to pry. Dusty maintained an unexplainable and uncomfortable feeling around Bill every time they met, but he always suppressed it enough to stay civil.

"You see anything odd on the road lately, any more coyote chewing on field spaghetti?" He questioned Dusty.

Last time he stopped to fill up, Dusty went on about seeing a coyote darting across the road with a snake flailing around in its jaws. "Nope, none Bill," Dusty replied, "but I did give a drifter a lift yesterday. She seemed nice, too. A dark-haired girl she was."

"I suppose you could say that's somewhat strange, we don't tend to see many rovers around these parts." Bill said with a clearly unimpressed look.

"True enough. It's rare that I see even one on the haul, let alone one willing to hop on." Dusty stated along with an emphatic shoulder shrug and simultaneous head scratch.

"Yep, did she ride with you for long?" Bill questioned.

"Oh, not too long really, she asked to be let out about sixty miles up the road. I didn't ask why, figured she might be weirded out by me." Dusty replied with a sense of frustration.

"Could be you spooked her, yep. Lost city girl running scared, probably grateful for the lift I reckon." Bill grinned back.

Then, a brief moment of silence was broken by the sound of the pump clicking to full. "Ah well. Yep, there is that at least. I did my part to help if she thinks I'm weird or not. What do I owe you?"

"Tab was taken care of last visit. You can run this one if you like." Bill suggested.

"Alright, thanks for that," replied Dusty. He then continued, "I best be off then, I still need to make it to Highrock tonight. I'll be back this way in a couple days if all works out."

By now, Maya located the abandoned farm and made her way to an old stone silo covered in creeping ivy next to a collapsed barn. The storm, which appeared quite bad from a distance, only managed to produce a vexatious light rain that didn't seem to want to let up.

Tall grass and bushy overgrowth enveloped the silo's base, mostly obscuring a decrepit wood door facing toward the field. Maya hops off the bike and walks it up to the silo door. With a good yank, the door nearly pulls it off the hinges as it creaks, but the solid wood remains intact.

The inside of the silo is only lit naturally by a small window at the top and through the opened door. A few old bales of hay are stacked off to the side while a broken metal ladder and a couple of old car tires are strewn about. Maya pulls the dirt bike inside, rests it against the hay bales, and puts her helmet on the handlebars.

She takes this opportunity to sit for a few minutes in the dry silo before continuing; she also uses the time to prepare for her flight. The survival knife, a few sundry items, and some cash will be left here.

While she is unsure if future plans lead her back to the silo, this at least provides benefit if they do. Plus, in keeping with a low profile, she really doesn't want attention from trying to bring the knife through airport security.

Unbeknownst to Maya, when she leaves the silo and starts heading into town, the dirt bike and helmet shimmer like heat-haze and transform into bales of hay.

Chapter 6

Monarch Beauty

Growing up, Jack watched and helped his parents on the farm, wrangling sheep, geese, and chickens. They poured a lot of hard work into the process to ensure the family prospers from each ounce of effort put in.

Hard labor invigorated the Kaona family, to the point they would feel restless and unable to sleep if a decent amount of work remained to be finished. There will always be chores to complete, this was well understood, but Jack yearned for a better way.

In his teens, Jack felt torn between help on the farm and duties on the farm. While realizing how much he contributes to the livelihood of the family, he grappled with a new-found addiction to education. The exciting universe of knowledge beckoned him, as if by name, to learn everything he possibly could to make lives better.

His parents were very much supportive of Jack's interest and encouraged him to find ways the knowledge could be applied.

"It's one thing knowing about a subject, but it's entirely different being able to apply a subject in the real world," his mother would say.

To which his father mirrored, "Exactly, and you will help more people if you can find ways to apply what you learn."

"If you know it well enough to teach it, you know it well enough to change the world," Jack's mother added.

The advice inspired Jack to look at ways he could change the world. At the time, that world is mostly made of schoolwork and helping out with the family farm.

At age fifteen, Jack's father taught him how to drive the tractor for crop harvest and plowing. This resulted in more time for his father to focus on other routine tasks and maintenance, which would also be passed down to Jack as his father becomes older.

There is certain serenity, a calming feeling of peace, driving a plow across fields for hours. Sometimes it took a little bit to get into the mode, but the mind is free to wander as soon as it hits.

Jack spent a lot of time thinking about life while driving the tractor. Eventually he reached an interesting conclusion, that if the tractor could plow the fields itself, he would have time to work on other endeavors.

It was then, when Jack formulated a plan to start making routine and repetitive tasks on the farm take care of themselves. He thought long and hard about how to automate daily chores so much that it became an obsession.

By age seventeen, Jack laid claim to his first invention and it's a doozy. He built an electric grid system around the fields that a tractor could use for positioning. Beacons on the fence pulse a signal into the air which the tractor picks up and decides what it should do based on the pattern.

The directive was simple to describe, but complex to create; A tractor keeps moving forward toward a beacon on one side of the field and then turns back toward an opposite beacon when the correct proximity is reached. It would then turn off at the last beacon and wait for someone to reset the program.

Jack's parents were absolutely astonished by what their son accomplished. They understood he wasn't trying to get out of chores, but instead using their advice to try and change the world by finding ways to help people.

Of course, his creation landed Jack's picture on the front page of a local paper, which turned into threats from big agriculture firms. His father helped Jack get a patent on the idea in attempt to secure his future. A rather large equipment supply company offered royalties in exchange for use of the patent and Jack started making income in a huge way.

He turned his sights on other processes around the farm with proceeds from the auto-plow. To complement harvesting, with a similar plow technology, Jack patented another device which picked up hay bales from the field, brought them to a barn, and stacked them in storage.

People following Jack's first invention now understood he's much more than just a one-hit-wonder; Jack becomes a phenome inventor and innovator before reaching twenty.

More royalties flooded into the bank with every invention; the development of automated farm devices quickly turned to passion. He was helping people and is profoundly changing the world.

Eventually, in his mid-twenties, Jack found a way to invent a concept he imagined a decade prior while watching his mother shear sheep. The process is an art she mastered, but it was taking a toll on her. A solution Jack contrived would prove to the world anything is possible.

Jack patented the world-famous Automatic Track and Shear. It's a device which locates a sheep ready for shearing using a radio frequency tag, shears it, and deposits the wool in a bin. This is a most bazaar sight to see, a machine roll across a field and gently clamp a sheep for trimming.

Animal activist groups first claimed cruelty upon seeing the machine in action, but Jack had a way to calm their concerns. He invited the groups over for live demonstrations and allowed them to get close with the robot during operation.

Complementing the auto-sheep machine, a second device grabbed wool from storage, ran it through a cleaning process, and produced bundles ready for use. Portions of the bundles were turned into yarn automatically and the remainder left for sale as is.

After seeing it, his mother pleaded, "Please don't automate the geese."

Jack found it amusing, in thought, to have a robot chase geese around to pluck down like something out of a cartoon show. He grinned at his mother and said, "Just for you, I will leave the geese be."

She laughed nervously and replied, "I know you can do it, you can do anything you put your mind to, but it's something I really enjoy as it is."

Uninterested in taking fun away from his mother, Jack moved to other inventions and kept his mother's words in the back of his mind. He went on to create over a hundred new devices while transforming the family farm into more of a luxury estate.

The push to create inventions slowed quite a bit when Jack met Julia. His focus shifted to one of love and deep, meaningful friendship. She made Jack happy as can be and helped him settle down while providing more direction in his life.

They met by chance at a hidden trail picnic area, on a rocky overlook, not far from his family farm. At first it seemed awkward, two solo hikers meeting at a place they each thought nobody else knew about, but a curious attraction brought them together.

A monarch butterfly fluttered its way across the picnic area, touching down briefly on cone flowers at the base of rocky outcrops along the way. Julia and Jack both noticed the butterfly's elegance as it slowly flapped while harvesting nectar from the flowers.

"She's beautiful, a true marvel of nature." Jack said in a calming voice.

Julia knew he was referring to the butterfly and couldn't help but think he might be talking about her in a passive way. She decided to assume he wasn't talking about her and instead tried to test him.

"How would you know she's a she?" Julia questioned inquisitively.

Jack replied instantly, "The butterfly? By the black spots on her hind wings and the webbing is more pronounced."

He paused for a moment and then felt brave enough to add, "It's very possible I was referring to you though."

Julia began blushing; this is definitely the most thoughtfully audacious compliment she's received in a lifetime. Normally a compliment like this from a stranger wouldn't take her the way it did, but the delivery provided a joyful tingling sensation which paired well with the fact she found him handsome.

She tilted her head down slightly, looked up at Jack and in a shy way and said, "You're quite the brave charmer for having just met me. May I be bold as well and tell you it's very possible your charm is working."

Julia wanted to hold the moment longer and turned towards the butterfly, "Do you find it amazing, how far a monarch will travel to stay warm?"

Jack is impressed, partly because Julia's comment feeds into his inner-geek, and it's a sort of knowledge committed to memory by interest in the subject.

"I am always amazed at the lengths nature will go to ensure continuity of life. By the way, my name is Jackson or Jack if you like," he replied with a nod and smile.

She happily responds, "Very true, nature always finds its way. My name is Julia and it's a pleasure to meet you, Jackson."

In a subtle effort to show Julia he has more depth than facts, Jack adds to the conversation, "I named the monarch as Maya, because the beauty on her outside is an illusion masking the trials and tribulations, she has endured to make it this far."

"I think it's a pretty name and I see what you mean. Sometimes people are easily glossed over, that is, what others have gone through to become who they are," Julia replies while also showing depth in understanding.

As quickly as it appeared, the monarch flew away from the overlook and into the valley to continue its journey. For a brief moment in its existence, unaware it was a subject of admiration.

A butterfly brought two people together who otherwise might have not broken the ice during this interaction. Given their penchant for knowledge however, and hiking in the same area, the probability is high they would have met again in the future.

Julia and Jack talked and talked for over an hour after first meeting. They realized a larger force, beyond conceivable control, brought them together one sunny afternoon in the forest. The weeks following were filled with hiking dates, a few dinners, and one breakfast together. Over time it became apparent – with all certainty – they are soul mates and would be together always.

When he felt comfortable, Jack introduced Julia to his parents and the strangely automated farm. She was flabbergasted by Jack's inventions and couldn't believe she didn't know who he was from publicity in the news. Then again, Julia didn't spend a lot of time watching television or keeping up with current events on the Internet; she is more interested in living life to its fullest.

An adventurer by every definition of the word, Julia loves to be outdoors as much as possible. She once worked as a trail guide helping novice hikers, and some seasoned veterans, to navigate challenging recreation trails in remote locations. During appropriate seasons, when extra help is always needed, she toured as a whitewater rapids instructor for all river skill levels.

Probably her most daring expedition would be crossing the Pacific Ocean by sailboat, alone, on a three-year journey. The trip placed Julia in a series of predicaments, such as catching sweeping winds on the outskirts of a hurricane, layovers on uncharted islands, and accidentally careening on hidden shoals' multiple times. She went into the adventure as a naive nineteen-year-old and exited a woman with fierce respect for the power and beauty of nature.

Kaona's farm though, has a magnetic personality of its own, and eventually Julia found ways in which the farm fulfilled her passion for the outdoors. As she settled down with Jack, by shifting priorities in life for those she cares about more, her lust of extreme adventures subsided to levels involving less stress and without the seriously risky levels of danger.

When it comes to adventures, the most daring outing for Jack was a hike to the summit of a nearby mountain. The terrain was rough and full of steep cliffs on either side of a narrow trail, which was maybe three to four feet wide at maximum. The weather, though favorable for the most part, turned ugly for a brief period during the climb and escalated the danger with slippery rocks.

He slowly pressed on, putting his destiny in the hands of the universe, and made it through. Arriving at the peak is a small achievement for professional hikers and a death wish for the inexperienced. He remained determined to see the summit, relish the moment, and then make his way home without a serious incident. The accomplishment would become a testament to Jack's will and perseverance.

Over a few years, while watching Julia's personality change subtly, Jack wondered if he took the roar out of the lioness. People change over time, it's as natural as any part of life, but he worried her thirst for the extreme would bubble-over one day from being suppressed for too long. Julia knew it was the right path forward, feeling more mature in the process, and reassured Jack that her days of sailing around the world had their moment to shine.

Their relationship, as meant to be, steadily progressed to marriage and Julia became pregnant shortly thereafter. Months later, when the special moment had arrived, Jack and Julia were both excited to see and hold their newborn miracle.

They patiently waited since mid-pregnancy to find out it was a healthy, beautiful baby girl by asking to have the ultrasound details kept secret unless there was a complication.

A short while after she gave birth, Julia asked Jack what he thought they should name her.

"Do you remember when we first met?" Jack asked.

With emotions recovering from the most naturally expressive moment of her life, Julia's eyes started to water a little, "I do, yes."

Her eyes mimicked those of a young version of herself, endearing and wide open with sincerity. She knew where he was heading with the question and it crossed her mind several times since first finding out she was going to be a mom.

Jack smiled as he gently picked up her free hand, which was resting beside her on the hospital bed, and enclosed it with both of his. With Julia, he found another way to change the world, by bringing life into it.

She added, "A monarch butterfly brought us together, there's no way I could forget."

"How about we name her Maya?" Jack replied with a smile as charming as the day they met.

Julia now has full-out tears of happiness gliding down her cheeks and is smiling pleasantly. She responds, "I still think it's a pretty name, she will become a beautiful monarch."

Her tears stopped, as though her mood suddenly changed, and motherly instinct kicked in.

"Isn't she adorable? Innocent, little Miss Maya Kaona," Julia states emphatically. She gently hugs baby Maya by pressing a soft, tearful cheek against her tiny face.

Then she looks at Jack, again with deep sincerity, and says, "I love you."

He warmly replies, "I love you!"

Chapter 7

Enum

It's about an hour walk along the municipal road in front of the abandoned farm to proximity of the airport. The rain gives Maya some cover in Lexton, making it less likely motorists will notice her, and she can keep her jacket hood up without looking too suspicious. She's skeptical over a plane ride also, thinking it's surely a bad idea if anyone is indeed looking for her.

At the airline counter, Maya pays cash for tickets for a local flight from Lexton to Norvil, and also an international flight from there to Istanbul. The return flight heads out of Istanbul three days later, back to Norvil, which eventually places her ten hours from Silverville. Three days gives Maya plenty of time to relax, visit Ash Hill, and return to Istanbul for her flight home.

Maya boarded her flight and used the time to catch up on much needed rest. The majority of passengers seemed to be in a similar state of mind, over-tired and relieved to let someone else guide the way for a while. After landing, Maya grabbed a local flight to Kayseri.

The short connecting flight from Istanbul was a more alive with alert passengers who visibly appeared anxious to touch down. It felt as though by the time the jet reached altitude, it was already approaching the tarmac.

In Kayseri, she rented a car with a card not linked to her, and then reserved a hotel room. Her plan for the evening is to have traditional Turkish Dürüm delivery and spend the remainder relaxing while sipping Rize tea. Though, a hot shower is number one on the list, especially after traipsing around the countryside and sleeping in stone bunkers.

Nighttime temperature hovered around the upper fifties, perfect to keep a window open for a breeze, and the sky remained clear throughout. With a glow of city lights, and faint shadow outline of Mount Erciyes in the distance, the view has an uncanny ability to allay almost anyone. In the morning, she woke up to the circular pattern print curtains flipping in the breeze over a wood end table.

Maya geared up and went downstairs for complimentary Kahvalti in a banquet room next to the lobby. She wrapped and packed a small plate of Börek into her pack tactical bag for later; then left the hotel, eating a Simit and carrying a coffee, while making her way to the rental car.

The drive to Ash Hill was very enjoyable under clear blue skies. Her excitement elevated as the ancient ruins popped into picture. Maybe it was Turkish coffee mixing with her anticipation, causing heart flutters, but finally she will be able to complete this part of the puzzle; or at least, so she thought.

Upon exiting the car, Maya heard a deep and thunderous rumble as the ground below her feet started to shake. She immediately looked at the ruins to see stones falling and small bursts of dust as pops and crackles filled the air. Then, the sands shifted ahead of her as a foot-wide fracture opened the surface.

She looked at the rift, tracing it backward to locate its origin. In the distance, a troublesome sight, Mount Erciyes is pushing a lofty plume of ash into the sky. Perhaps overdue, the last time this stratovolcano erupted was over nine thousand years ago.

"Oh, this is diverting." She says.

Time is clearly of the essence. Maya rushed to the ruins, jumped over the fault, and worked her way to the Station-7 GPS coordinates; pointing to a three-foot pillar of stone standing on its own without walls or foundation blocks in the vicinity.

A side of the pillar contains an inscription while the other surfaces were smoothed off. There is a problem, however. Maya doesn't know how to read cuneiform script and the letters on the pillar are chiseled with a series of symbols and lines.

Then she recalled her GPS backup plan, a piece of paper and pencil. Both items were stuffed into an expandable side pocket on her tactical bag days ago. She pulls the paper out and places it over the cuneiform pillar. Using the pencil on its side, she presses in and rubs to transfer the texture to paper.

Without knowing if the Erciyes eruption might intensify, Maya elects to not risk going to Kayseri. She decides to drive to Istanbul and avoid the overly alert commuter flight. The worry now is whether or not the flight to Norvil will be cancelled if the ash plume starts heading toward Istanbul.

Maya drove with impetuosity away from Ash Hill while the smoke plume seemed to shrink over time in her rearview mirror. The cuneiform pillar shook and sunk into the sand as a second crack opened under the site. Several hours passed, sunlight turned into shadow, and Maya made it to Istanbul.

Like the plane ride to Turkey, the trip back to Norvil was routine, except for one instance in particular. Maya woke from a nap to attendants moving up and down the aisle for mid-flight meal service. She pulled out the cuneiform etching and placed it on the lap tray in front of her. The shapes and lines made patterns that she couldn't quite recognize.

"Maya, is it, yes?" says a female voice with a French accent.

Maya turned around and a flight attendant, named Sofia, was looking directly at the piece of paper. "How did you know my name?" Maya asked after not recognizing the attendant.

"Your name is Maya?" Sofia questioned. Maya's face was puzzled and then Sofia pointed to the cuneiform paper to say, "The cuneiform says Maya too, you see?"

Astonished by her ability, Maya asked the flight attendant, "Do you know cuneiform?"

Sofia smiled and responded, "I studied archaeology in Kayseri before flying on planes, yes. I didn't get to uh, travel much yes, so then I decided to become a hostess, you see."

Maya knew all too well about that aspect of archaeology. "I agree, life is best when you love what you're doing, right?" she said without trying to be too cliché.

"Why yes of course, Maya. Would you like a soda or some pretzels?" Sofia questioned.

Maya elected to have a soda. The feeling of carbonated beverages and chewing ice at altitude puts her at ease in a pressurized cabin. After the refreshment, she closed her eyes for the last half of the flight to rest.

Sofia translating the cuneiform script saved Maya time otherwise spent searching electronic libraries to piece letters together. The translation must be a code for something else, she thought, because it didn't make sense when combined with two halves of the algorithm already obtained. A secret lab in Norvil will soon answer this question and Maya was almost there.

The plane touched down in the late evening without delay. Hanging televisions in the terminal played breaking news coverage of Mount Erciyes as Maya walked by. By the looks of the fallout, she was right to leave Ash Hill instead of heading back to Kayseri.

From the airport, Maya hailed a taxi to the Norvil business district and asked to be let out at a coffee shop. Travel with irregular sleep is starting to catch up with her, but a little caffeine will perk things up for a while.

Maya walks to the heart of downtown with her hood up and head tilted forward but not quite looking down. Her hair wraps around her face and bounces outward in sync with each step. Every so often she passes by others walking and chooses to remain observant without acknowledgement; it's a defensive tactic she reverts to in big cities at night.

Stimuli in the city can overwhelm Maya at times, especially when she's under a bit of stress. Several characters, either passing by or standing at what seems to be random locations, often appear shady even if they're probably not interested in Maya's presence at all. She keeps walking, sipping her coffee, and making her way forward.

Upon arriving at the building, Maya uses a side entrance in the alley which is normally meant for business tenant deliveries. The hallway leads to a set of elevators with the option to visit the front desk on the way past. Security cameras document people coming and going over three-day periods; however, the camera wiring was tapped into by Jack after moving into the fifth-floor offices.

Her father's most sophisticated technology lab, named Station-5, contains an array of systems he built for a variety of research. To remain under the radar, he leveraged a hidden in plain sight strategy. The lab occupies floor five of the Norvil Trust investment building and is disguised as a digital web security and athenaeum operation.

Entry from the elevator is controlled by a jet-black foyer door with biometric security. A dark gray reception desk next to the doorway is usually empty. The hallway flooring and walls are black as well, with a subtle seamless blue marble swirl pattern throughout. A thin blue light, in the shape of a wave, splits the wall horizontally at eye-level.

Inside, the decor favors a pure white theme to help amplify light while remaining free from any color spectrum influence. There are several hermetically sealed rooms with no visible doors or windows. Each room is black inside, according to documentation, and contains a framework grid for controlled experiments only accessible from the master control room. Forced entry into any room triggers a self-destruct mechanism.

Maya proceeds to the control room, which has a visible door, and provides a finger print and retina scan to enter. A glass monitor is bolted to a wall inside like a projection screen.

The huge monitor looks like a computer in hibernation, with a similar blue wave pattern as the foyer, pulsating gently across the screen. As she steps closer to the screen, it wakes up and greets her. "Hello Maya."

"Your father verified your identity for me some time ago." The machine stated in a distinctly human voice. "You may identify me as, Enum, which is short for enumeration. I am a collection of constants." Enum then paused for a moment.

"Hi, Enum, it's good to meet you." Maya replied while attempting to assuage her disbelief.

Enum recognized Maya's jitters and set to calm her by beginning the master protocol. "Maya, you are here for training exercises, to learn how to wield power soon entrusted to you. Here, you will navigate seven universes for the next evolutionary leap."

The screen switches to display a wireframe model of a room with what appears to be a black hole in the center. Enum continues introducing the system. "Each room on this floor contains a wormhole transport to a parallel universe. These, together, are only seven of an infinite number of possible outcomes. Your father, Jack Kaona, built the tunnels and machines capable of interacting with them."

A view of life on planet Earth plays on the screen as Enum continues. "Entering a wormhole will subject you to a new reality that can be similar or very different than the one you know now. Your conscious, and sub consciousness, attune without intervention."

Maya is contemplative at a level of marvel beyond anything she's ever experienced. What her father built is beyond anything imagined by the greatest minds to have existed on Earth. Always theories, but this proves a lot more than theory. "How is it possible?" She asked Enum.

"Think of it this way, Maya. The reality you know now will always be your home universe and you may travel to others without fear of disrupting your home reality. Your father traveled through thousands of wormholes and brought knowledge home each time. He created scenario universes simply by altering only one thing from his home reality and then traveled to a dimensional plane to witness the scenario unfold." Enum responded.

"This is amazing! I am beyond words even remotely capable of describing a fraction of it. Can you tell me, are there any consequences?" Maya asked the collection of constants.

"By definition, any action has consequence. I am still unsure why humans tend to associate a consequence with a sense of dread." Enum replied.

The machine continued, "If you meant by consequence, that bad may happen from travel to another universe, the answer is yes. However, this only holds true in universes you visit. Your home universe will stay as you left it, except time will not pass while you are away and you will not age."

Maya looks for clarification over the impact of her actions and asks Enum, "Is there anything I should be worried about based on decisions made in other universes then?"

Images of life on a planet similar to Earth fade into havoc on the glass screen. Enum pauses for a short moment for a calculated response and then says. "While your actions in other universes do not affect your home universe, you will likely experience moral emotion over shadows left in your wake. However, it is wise to consider your actions in another universe as one of an infinite number of potential outcomes which would have happened regardless of instigation."

Enum finishes the introduction by stating, "Under certain limitations of this matrix, you may experience glitches or blips in dimensional fabric. Rest assured, however, this is quite normal. Maya, I have finished the overview and standby for your commands. There is no limit to the time you may take to think things over. The overview may be repeated when requested. Please state you're ready when you'd like to begin."

Chapter 8

Thunderhead

Bright, ivory light pierced the Kaona's farm house, flooding every room with beams of radiant energy. Dust particles, which otherwise wouldn't be visible to a naked eye, are swirling in feather-like eddies as a slight cross-breeze flows through open windows.

Air flow fluctuates from almost stagnant to nearly too much at a time, and the sudden changes are temporary effects from bad weather on the horizon. Maya's grandfather, Boyd, is snoring in a recliner and unaffected by the gusty winds.

A slow-moving storm is rolling in from the mountains and tracking directly at the farm house. The front is pushing strong winds ahead of it while dragging along a curtain of rain soon to envelope the farmstead. It's a rare occurrence for a storm this strong to head directly at the farm and the Kaona's are frantically buttoning down everything possible to minimize damage.

Julia is busy preparing the goose coops by fastening entry doors to the ground to keep them from flying off. The coops are secured to small cement pads and those platforms have safety eye-bolts protruding near the door area. She needs to run a hook-end strap across the door, latch it on the eye-bolts and tighten. With a number of coops to attend to, the process is taking Julia longer than she expected.

Jack is inside a small shed off to the side of the house, running equipment systems diagnostics and monitoring incoming weather. He is hopeful the storm will bring lightning for a bizarre and crazy experiment meant to capture it in a bottle. The apparatus is on a hill one mile from the farm with a live-feed camera recording the action.

Oblivious of the storm's magnitude, Maya sits on the living room couch, reading a book on philosophy that's well beyond her age-level. She is only ten years old and already understands more about the world than a lot of adults three times her age.

Grandmother Tabby is putting away dishes in the kitchen after lunch. She takes time to dry every plate and piece of silverware thoroughly with the intent of putting all of her effort into the process even if some might consider it mundane. Tabatha is a stickler for cleanliness, almost to the point of an obsessive-compulsive disorder.

The storm continues to creep across the sky, closer and closer to the farm. Wind gusts whip through the air more violently than before and nearly rip off the window blinds. Tabatha became increasingly concerned about the weather when she noticed the sky darkening from the kitchen window.

"Maya, be a dear and please close up those two windows before the blinds fly off their tracks," Tabatha directed.

"I'm going to run outside and make sure your parents are heading back, it looks like this storm isn't going to blow over," She added.

"Yes, grandma," replied Maya with a strong tone of politeness.

Maya placed her book upside-down on the couch to use the cushion as a bookmark and then walked over to close the windows.

Tabatha went to see her son, Jack, since he was closest to the house. The wind wrestled with her clothing as she crossed the yard to the equipment shed. Jack was right in the midst of packing a few things up.

"How bad does it look?" Tabatha asked.

Jack smiled and replied, "Bad, probably not bad enough for the storm cellar, thankfully. I was just heading over to check on Julia and then back to the house."

"Alright, I just wanted to check and make sure everything is fine. I'm going to head back to the house then. Your father is asleep in the chair again," Jack's mother said.

"Everything is fine, mom. I'll go get Julia and we'll be right there," Jack said.

Tabatha went back to the house and once again fought the wind on her way. Jack walked with her part way and then turned into the field for a short ten-minute hike to the geese area. He looked ahead, directly into the wind, and couldn't spot Julia outside anywhere; she went into the storage outbuilding a moment before Jack started his walk.

The storm clouds rolling in spread across the sky and blocked the sun from illuminating the path ahead. He pulled out a pocket flashlight and flipped it on to see his way. Strobes of lightning lit up everything with a quick white flash, followed by loud cracks of thunder resonating deep enough to vibrate windows and glassware in the house.

Jack made it to the building a few minutes later to find Julia sitting at a desk with the weather radar on.

"Did you get everything situated here?" He asked.

Julia replied with a partial look of panic, "All set, yes. There is a lot of red heading this way with a few bands of purple."

"Not to worry, let's get back to the house before," Jack replied and paused.

Large drops of rain started hitting the building's tin roof like a bucket in the sky tipped over to let globs of water escape at a time.

"Before the rain hits," he continued.

Julia grinned, "Yea, I think we're a bit late for that now."

They left the outbuilding and started the trek back to the house. A service light above the doorway emphasized the slant of incoming rain as streams of water skipped across the lit area. Julia pulled out a giant umbrella and pushed it open to cover from the weather. She's always prepared and looks out for Jack whenever possible, which is part of why he loves her as much as he does.

"I love you, dear. I thought the rain would hold off longer and didn't bring one, but I have a flash light," Jack said as Julia raised the umbrella.

"Love you too! I figured it might be needed and good thing for the light," she replied.

The sound of rain drops bouncing off the umbrella fabric is louder than standing under the tin roof. Despite the size of the umbrella, both Jack and Julia were still getting soaked from the waist down by sideways rain. They picked up the pace with little desire to be caught outside during the worst of the storm.

"Did you see that? It's a piece of hail!" Julia said excitedly while pointing at a small ball of ice.

Jack quickly noticed another one hit the grass, "Over there too, here it comes."

The deep patter of rain on the umbrella became even louder as shards of hail began hitting it. One piece went through the fabric, midway between the edge and main support handle, and created a hole which caused some of the rain to pour inside instead of rolling down to the edge.

"Look, one went through the umbrella!" Julia said as they both noticed the incident.

"We're almost there, hopefully the cover holds up another five minutes."

They arrived at the house and went inside. Grandma Tabby set out candles everywhere which transformed the interior into something out of an eerie Halloween tale. Jack laughed quietly when he noticed all of the candles.

"Ma, what's with all of the candles? We have a backup generator, trust me, it will kick-on if needed," Jack said.

"Well, you never know, Jackson. We're getting hail the size of rum balls out there!" She replied with slight nervousness in her voice.

Right after she spoke, before Jack could reply, the lights went out and the house stood still in silence. The hum from electricity disappeared completely; the kind of silence where instinct tells someone it's a bad situation. Fortunately, it's a good thing Tabatha set out the candles for light because the generator did not kick-on.

Jack knew something major was wrong the moment the house went dark. His custom power redundancy system is seamless and designed to fail-over with only a little flicker in the lights.

"I guess we do need the candles after all. I'm going to check the system out though, we should have power," Jack said.

Tabatha smiled at her accomplishment and at the notion Jack admitted to.

There are two connections for the backup power system, one in a basement panel for power in, and the other from the generator in a small room attached to the electronics shed. Jack went to the basement first to see if the fault was there.

Everything looked normal in the panel aside from a voltage throughput reading, which showed barely that of a potato or lemon. The low voltage confirmed continuity between the shed and the house.

Jack went back upstairs and over to the living room where Tabatha, Julia and Maya were talking. Grandpa Boyd appeared to still be sleeping in the recliner.

"We're not getting power into the house. I'm going to go check in the shed," He said with concern.

At least he had a few service lights on solar battery backup to see his way around. In the shed, Jack noticed a surge protector on the generator had a red light indicating a fault.

A power surge tripped the breaker, but it didn't make sense to Jack; the system is grounded to prevent a surge feeding back along the main line. He punched the breaker and the generator started up for a second, then sputtered out and tripped again.

"Do we have fuel?" Jack questioned while unscrewing the reservoir tank cap.

"No."

He grabbed a large fuel jug from a stack of cans in the corner of the generator room. After filling up the tank, Jack punched the surge switch once again. The generator turned over and roared to life with a sound loud enough to muffle rain hitting the shed roof. His monitoring equipment booted up and lights turned back on in the house.

"There we go."

He went over to the house, back into the living room and said, "I can't believe I overlooked that."

"No gas?" Julia asked with a snicker.

"Yep, I can't believe I didn't check it during prep," he replied.

Tabatha smiled and said sarcastically, "You figured it out though and now we have lights, so much for the romantic candlelight."

Julia finished her thought with sympathy, "It's always something simple."

"You can leave the candles burning, be sure to snuff them out so we don't have a fire to deal with too," Jack said.

Suddenly, Grandpa Boyd woke from his slumber and slumped to the floor while clutching the left side of his chest. He took a few short gasps before passing out on his side.

Jack immediately responded to the action without hesitation, "Julia, give him CPR, he's gone into cardiac arrest and not breathing. I'm calling for help."

Tabatha and Julia, who are both in shock, ran over to Boyd. They rolled him on his back and Julia began administering CPR. Tabatha helped count and did her best to fight emotion. Maya had tears gliding down her face while watching helplessly. The storm continued to downpour as the thunderhead passed over.

Julia and Tabatha each took turns using their basic resuscitation training knowledge before emergency response arrived. The medics quickly assessed the situation, began defibrillation, and pushed a round of epinephrine.

Jack scurried to get a few things together to leave, knowing things were not going well.

"Maya, go get your coat, please," He said.

Julia took a cue and prepared to leave into town. Before getting her purse and coat, she pulled a candle snuffer out of a junk drawer in the kitchen and handed it to Maya.

"Here, go put out the candles and meet us in the car," She told her.

Responders could not get a pulse to return and moved quickly to rush Boyd to the hospital. The tall one took off outside and returned with a stretcher and transport. They rolled Grandpa Boyd onto the board, lifted him onto the stretcher, and rolled the stretcher out the door to the ambulance. Tabatha practically forced her way to his side.

One of the paramedics told her, "Normally there isn't room to ride along in this bus when we need to continue our work. Sit up there and give us room to work, please."

The second paramedic looked at the first with a mixed expression, thinking about how rude the bluntness sounds, but understood his point.

Jack, Julia and Maya followed behind the ambulance into town.

During the drive, things appeared grim to Jack, as he stared ahead at red and white flashing lights blaring through the rain. Julia worried too, knowing Jack's father had been warned about his health conditions and how he refused to make any lifestyle changes.

Maya is in the back seat, curled up against the side door, looking out the window in despair with wetness from the rain masking her tears. She is taking the event harder than everyone else, as though it's her fault; it's not easy to be so young and witness a tragedy happen to a loved one, let alone understand exactly what's happening.

Julia addressed the situation in a calming voice, "I know this isn't easy for you, Maya. It isn't easy for us either. Everything works out for the best, even if it doesn't seem like it at the time."

The words of wisdom failed to pull Maya away from staring through the car window. She is young, but understands the severity of the situation from a medical diagnosis book she read out of interest in the subject; a further testament to Maya's ability to understand the world at an early age.

Maya's intelligence quotient is higher than above normal on the testing spectrum. At least two doctors have tried to get parental consent to run a series of experiments with her, to identify why she is at a savant level of intelligence, but her parents refuse to let it happen.

Paramedics worked diligently to try and save Grandpa Boyd as their immediate directive. Partway through transport to the hospital, they received a note from Boyd's physician with orders to not resuscitate and were forced to stop recovery efforts at that point.

Tabatha knew her husband had a DNR in place and understood it was only a matter of time before paramedics would be ordered to cease. She prepared for this moment for years, starting with the first incidents of health decline and Boyd's stubbornness, but she still has trouble coming to terms with the reality of it.

Despite losing her best friend, Tabatha was relieved Boyd is now free from a progressively worsening condition. True to his personality, Boyd vehemently refused angioplasty surgery, citing no doctor should interfere with the natural order of life.

Boyd's doctor knew he could not otherwise reverse damage caused from multiple ischemic strokes and suggested lifestyle improvements to hopefully give Boyd more time. Toxic molecules from brain strokes triggered cardiac cell death and eventual heart attack.

Jack learned about his father's distaste for medical treatment while growing up in the family. Nothing short of a stroke would bring Boyd to see a doctor – he even elected to set his own arm after breaking it in a fall at age thirty-five.

The family accepted Boyd's refusal to see doctors and dentists because there was really no way to change his mind on the matter; they could not force him to go against his will. Furthermore, Jack was completely unaware his father made a standing order to not resuscitate, but he wouldn't be surprised to find out given the history.

Julia looked at Jack with an expression of concern, placed a hand over his, and let him know she is there for him without words. The tension turned to silence as minds raced through the worst possible scenarios. The sounds of echoing sirens and rain from the passing storm filled the car with an ominous feeling.

Then, the worst thing for Jack to see at this moment, the speeding ambulance slowed down and turned off its emergency lights. Julia squeezed Jack's hand and tears rolled down her face.

Jack looked over at Julia and exchanged the same look from her before; knowing time had finally run out for his dear old father.

He looked towards the backseat at Maya and said, "Maya, honey, it looks like they're calling it – Grandpa isn't going to make it."

Maya's face filled with sadness, "It will be alright, he has a new purpose now."

Julia teared up a little more, not only from the substance of Maya's comment, but also at the level of maturity for her age.

She replied, "Yes, we all move on to better places in the end, Maya, you are right. Grandpa is in a better place now."

Jack is quiet in the driver's seat, following the lifeless ambulance while trying to hold back his emotions. He wants to appear strong and able to hold things together when the worst of life can happen as it does. Losing his father is upsetting, though a fact of life, but he is also concerned about how his mother is holding up.

"I really hope mom is alright, I can't even imagine," Jack said.

Julia replied with confidence, "She will be alright in time, you know she is a strong woman."

"I know, and I've heard the phrase before, that life wouldn't put anyone in a situation they're not capable of overcoming. I worry though, she may be tough, but she is still human," Jack pauses.

"They were together for a long time, and fifty-three years at that. It won't be easy once the initial shock wears off and loneliness sets in."

Julia attempts to set some reason to Jack's worries, "Try thinking about what we can do now for her, one thing at a time, and we can work on the rest later if it happens."

Chapter 9

Memory

From a very early age, Maya demonstrated an adaptive learning ability which baffled most people who met her. One peculiar skill intrigued even those skeptical of her intelligence – She could recall events in vibrant detail as though the scene was unfolding before her very eyes at the moment. Those with a slight understanding did not call it photographic memory, but instead referred to the skill as motion-graphic recall; rather than seeing memories as pictures, she sees video.

Maya started walking at seven months old and didn't begin to talk until nearly two years after her first steps. Jack and Julia were concerned at first and then decided it was best for her to follow her own pace. Tabatha's advice noted how Jack was also a late talker and how she believes it made him more of a thinker; perhaps the same applied to Maya.

A portion of Maya's enhanced intelligence broke free when she finally started talking. Her first word was "discombobulating" as mimicked and she repeated it over and over again until her voice sounded just like Julia's when originally heard.

During health check-ups, Maya reminded her doctor of everything that happened during the last visit in detail. This is when her physician first noticed Maya may have an extraordinary ability, to be able to recite all as it was without forgetting a detail. The doctor could even ask about placement of supplies, staged purposefully months prior to see if she would remember, and Maya knew.

Word of her talent traveled quickly through the community, and before too long, in the ears of an intelligence agency known as FIS. The agency sought to procure Maya's ability and replicate it for top secret operations by attempting to gain parental consent for her participation in various covert programs.

Jack and Julia felt something was off when agents showed up at the farm unannounced while posing as research doctors. Maya's parents didn't know who the supposed doctors were working for and often found logical fallacies in reasoning they used for coaxing an agreement. Instead, Jack and Julia would politely ask them to leave.

Maya eventually learned how to control her ability and prevented situations like those in the doctor's office from happening again. Her parents formulated a plan to disguise the gift from agents by having Maya show less and less recall ability. After some time, she was no longer of interest and they stopped randomly showing up.

Researchers in FIS theorized that Maya's recall skill only existed at an impressionable age and thought childhood mental development had displaced the area of her brain enabling motion-graphic recall. Meanwhile, growing older allowed Maya to understand her ability and mask it if need be, especially with reasoning from her parents.

For many years, Maya understood her life to be a frustrating battle between letting beauty inside flourish and suppressing it from existing. She enjoyed how happy her abilities could make people, but strongly disliked anyone who tried to take advantage of her and felt it was best to keep her intelligence locked away.

One day, after the years of soul searching and observation, Maya finally realized there are a number of people who seek to take advantage of others and her abilities don't change that fact. She envisioned this behavior as a survival tactic, when certain personality types learn to survive by any means necessary without moral objection.

As she found ways to separate opportunists from those after ability, Maya began to question why she was blessed with a gift she couldn't share with the world. She looked inward with thinking exercises to try and understand, but a wall in her subconscious prevented an answer from flowing to the surface.

Maya's philosophical thoughts resemble a life-long struggle many philosophers grapple with, in the questioning of existence in its entirety. Why are we here? What happens when we die? It's easy for her to ask these questions repeatedly without progress, as they tend to feed an unrelenting cycle of understanding; until a moment when she finally found way to make sense of life.

The more she read between lines, the more it allowed her to see life in a completely different light. Maya worked with her brain waves, instead of against them, and asked only a single question to see the universe offer a solution. When it did, the solution presented in a most unexpected way – answers appear indirectly by association, which would be easy for anyone to gloss over without notice if they happened upon it by accident.

Possibly the most interesting point about Maya's perception isn't how she notices answers between lines, but rather how her father exhibited the same thought patterns at a young age. Jack also found creditability in subtleties the universe provided and believed those patterns existed to help him through tough problems.

Sometimes the messages to Maya, or Jack, were filled with substance unrelated to questions they desired answers for. In one example, Maya asked about the meaning of life and spent the next day fixated on people wearing glasses. Instead of the universe answering the meaning of life, it put emphasis on the fact Maya needed to readjust her focus; at least, this is how she understood it.

As she grew older, and learned more about the world, Maya started to realize even simple answers are a complicated process for the universe to unpack. She developed sympathy and guilt over asking too much of the universe. Out of respect, she stopped asking questions relentlessly and let the universe guide her instead.

Part of why she decided it is best to have the universe be her guide, rather than a personal answer-book, relates to the days when Maya first developed feelings for boys. One day, during an afternoon physical education class, she became suddenly obsessed with a boy and couldn't explain irrational feelings taking over methodic thought process.

Maya craved to know, almost as much as she craved the boy, how he could distract her from everything without interaction; or why she felt like throwing up while standing next to him in a recess line. She reverted back to asking the universe for specific answers and was not happy about what it showed her.

When she found enough courage to talk to the boy during one recess, Maya witnessed him kissing another girl. At first it seemed harmless, until Maya suddenly realized strange new feelings she had, disappointment and jealousy. Then she wondered why the universe would answer her with those feelings from such an innocent question.

It didn't take long after her first crush and tiny heartbreak to recognize what the universe was trying to say. Maya wanted to know why she had these boy-crazy feelings and the universe showed her a glimpse of what those feelings become. The event disappointed Maya because she found out why from a distance, but did not get to experience it first-hand.

In retrospect, with virgin feelings involved, she preferred an example over trying to figure it out with no prior knowledge. The incident taught Maya many new things about life, and helped her understand why it's better to ask for guidance instead of direct answers. It might have turned out differently if Maya had asked, "Can that boy over there tell me why I feel like I do about him?"

A shy girl in seventh grade happened to see Maya's excitement deflate from a distance and felt like she needed to say something. She approached to comfort and told Maya, "They're only boys you know."

She giggled, and said, "Hi! I'm Cassy."

Maya was a bit startled by the voice behind her, "Oh hello! I'm Maya, and what do you mean, only boys?"

"They really don't know what they want, that's what my mom tells me," replied Cassandra.

She paused for a second with a giggle and a little dance, "They're young and confused because they noticed girls for the first time."

"I'm also confused. I feel like I just noticed him for the first time too," said Maya.

"Mom said it's normal at this age for a girl to be confused by boys being confused. She also said I should find a friend to talk about boys with when she's not home to talk to. Do you want to be my friend?" Cassandra asked.

Maya grinned, "Yes! You're my first real friend, Cassandra. It's nice to meet you."

A few years passed from this moment, the very same moment Maya would flash back to every now and then when she missed Cassandra. They became very close friends, sharing everything with each other, until the pivotal and tragic day when Maya's life changed forever.

Nearly a year after Cassandra obtained her driver's permit; they went driving at night along the countryside. Cool and crisp air outside is a nice temperature to have the windows rolled down for, and the sky is filled with twinkling stars. The girls were talking about boys and family issues, similar to when they first met.

Cassandra followed concession side roads for a while and then hopped on a pretty winding drive running parallel to a river. The road is above the river with a slight drop to the shoreline. Soon enough though, the two girls would find out the drop isn't as slight as it looks at night.

On a curve bending left, Cassandra was too engulfed by a conversation on family trouble and missed her turn. The car plowed straight forward, off the road, and down the embankment into the river. Cassandra hit her head badly on the steering wheel when the car plunged into the water; her airbag failed to deploy and she was knocked out.

Maya wasn't paying a lot of attention to the road either. The conversation was upsetting and frustrating because Cassandra's parents expected her to leave for college in a year. Maya knew that Cassandra wanted to wait back for a year or two to figure out if college is the right path. She was going to offer to get an apartment with her, but then she realized they were about to hit water.

Just before impact, Maya wanted to stay silent because she didn't want the last noise she heard to be screams. Meanwhile, oddly enough, Cassandra's involuntary reflex caused an inaudible scream to stay trapped in her stomach.

The passenger airbag deployed and saved Maya from hitting the dashboard directly. She was conscious and uninjured from impact, but noticed Cassandra's head-bobbing off to one side with blood running from a wound into the water. She realized the river was quickly pouring in the open car windows and had to act fast.

She undid her seatbelt and then reached over to Cassandra to free her from the restraint. She gently turned Cassandra in her seat, as best as possible, to get her back facing the driver's side door. Maya then escaped through the passenger window and swam over to the driver's side to get Cassandra.

Maya put an arm across and under both of Cassandra's arms, and then attempted to brace her while pulling her from the car. She took Cassandra to the shore and rolled her on her side. Right before Maya was going to start resuscitation, Cassandra's eyes opened and she coughed up some water. She is awake, but confused and disorientated.

Thankful she didn't lose it in the accident; Maya pulled out her phone from a zippered cargo pant pocket and dialed for help. She kept an eye on Cassandra's breathing and talked to her about fond memories they shared while waiting for help to arrive.

At the hospital, Maya finished injury screening and went to see her best friend resting comfortably in a private patient room. Cassandra woke from the footsteps as Maya approached.

"You hit your head pretty good. How are you feeling now?" Maya asked in a soft voice.

Cassy replied, "Better than a few hours ago, that's for sure."

"It's a good thing we weren't both knocked out," responded Maya.

"Hot doctor, Dr. Bryce, said I'm recovering nicely. It's a mild brain contusion and I have to take it easy for a few days."

Cassandra recalled moments leading up to the crash and tried to process what happened. Maya placed a hand over Cassy's left hand, which was clutching at the hospital blanket like she was still gripping the steering wheel. Maya took the moment in silence to deal with her memory from earlier flashing back.

"You saved me. I remember you saved me from drowning or something. I woke up choking on the beach and couldn't figure out how I ended up there, soaked, after driving the moment before – it felt instantaneous. I don't know how I could ever thank you." Cassy stated.

Maya responded with emotion, "The car was filling with water. I just reacted to the situation and I know you would have done the same for me. I didn't know if you were paralyzed or not by the way your head was leaning, but I knew we needed to get out of the car fast. You were coming and going."

Cassandra smiled and slightly relaxed her hand gripping the blanket. She is happy to be alive, but nervous at the same time because she remembered what her and Maya were chatting about right before the accident.

"Do you remember what we were talking about? You were getting pretty worked up about it, I understand why, and I was about to tell you something before we hit the river," Maya said as she couldn't keep it in any longer.

"I do, I'm sorry, it shouldn't have distracted me so much that we both ended up in danger," replied Cassy.

Maya went back to the conversation like the accident was already well in the past, which in a way was true, because both girls acknowledged it happened and preferred not to dwell; they preferred to focus on the future and understand the past cannot be changed.

"Well, I wanted to let you know then, but maybe you can stay back a year or two before college and we can get an apartment. That way you don't have to worry about being kicked out from your place and we'll get to hang out every day."

"You know how cool and fun that would be?" Cassy responded with excitement.

"Yes!"

"I can't do it, I'm sorry, Maya."

"Why not, I thought maybe..."

"Well, you know Jeff, right?"

"Yes."

"He and I want to travel abroad for a while, what with my parents giving me the boot and all," Cassandra stated.

"Oh, I see. That will be cool and fun too, right?" Maya asked.

"It's nice of you to offer, but I was about to tell you before driving off the road like a buffoon."

Maya's eyes started to water a little, "I almost lost you and now I'm going to miss you."

"I know sweetie, I'm going to miss you like crazy too. It's difficult for me to imagine life without being able to see you," replied Cassandra.

"Do you trust him enough to live abroad with?"

"With all of my heart I do."

"Good, I want you to be safe. You'll have to write, call or text often, within reason I guess," Maya said.

A devious look washed over Cassy's face.

"Hey, I'm not going just yet. I haven't told him yes, but I did pull my job savings out of the bank. Let's have a going-away party then, so we can have some fun before Jeff and I leave."

A few months passed after the accident and Cassandra hosted a really entertaining going-away party as anticipated. Then, in what seemed like a blink of an eye, she was on her way and Maya felt alone for the first time in years. Cassandra was her best friend and pretty much her only friend since they met.

Chapter 10

In the Void

Questioning everything is a passion for my dad, which sometimes gets in the way of progress. He desires to understand exactly how things work and uses the knowledge for invention. Whether creating or innovating a device, Jack definitely enjoys solving problems so much that he allows it consume all aspects of his life.

My father is a good beginning for this entry in the Chronicles of Shadow. He is the principal inspiration for my involvement in future events, but I will volunteer the fact my mother is a vital influence too. They raised me with the freedom to be who I am, for my decisions to matter, without trying to push me into something I am not.

The family farm, which my father also grew up on, was inherited from his parents shortly after I was born. Jack's parents found they were unable to keep up with physical demands of the farm and asked him to take over. They didn't want to move away from the countryside and offered help with raising me, to which my parents welcomed.

Somehow, he found time between farming commitments to foster his, and my own, interest in education. My father wanted me to understand technology as an extension of nature instead of a nemesis. Many of his private patents introduced forms of environmentally conscious automation to the family farm, which in turn freed up more time to spend with the family.

My grandparents spent quite a bit of time with us before they both passed away from natural causes. When it happened, we finally understood how close they really were. His father passed first, then his mother a week later. They spent every day together, and in the end, they still couldn't bear to be apart.

They encouraged my father with anything he chose to do even if they didn't fully understand, and here we are today. Likewise, my mother was very supportive as far as I can remember. If they had any marital problems, it's difficult to really know from what I witnessed growing up.

My mother was a very hard worker, like my father, and also spent a lot of time with family. She has this uncanny ability to make you happy even as she is no longer with us. Many of my memories depict her smiling as she toils away on whatever it happened to be at the time. Perhaps in a way my memories are biased, or her mouth just naturally formed a smile, but I see it as something pleasant; to be able to picture her enjoying life.

I remember one conversation with her that is right up there in terms of witnessing who she really is on a personal level. In my teen years, one Saturday, we were sitting in the farm house living room having tea.

"Maya, you can be anything you want if you put your mind to it." She told me.

The midafternoon sun pierced white lace drapes and illuminated the room, blanketing over the wood floors, furniture, and the old dusty area rug next to our couch. At times you could see dust particles floating in the air where the sun rays were thickest.

An aggressive, breeze knocked the drapes around, which caused them to make a light airy noise letting everyone know what the weather's like from inside. We could hear birds and insects enjoying the weather outside of the window.

What started the conversation is when I asked her, or rather complained, about how some things in life don't seem fair. She responded to me saying, "We are part of a unique existence, Maya. Whether our individual roles are small or large in our own judgement, each of us is just as important as the next. You might look at another person, and think they are better off than you, but they are only fulfilling a different role."

"How would one know if they are fulfilling their role? It's not how the universe responds to me specifically or lets me know if I'm doing a good job, or not." I said to her with doubt; and I truly felt it was impossible know.

My mother took a sip of tea and responded, "You're an intelligent young adult. You know you can be anything you want to be and the universe will help make it happen – there is no limit to your abilities."

She paused for a moment to let that sink in and then continued, "The universe, and god, let people know they're on the right path all the time. What is essential to remember, is recognizing how it's being told to you."

"I have an example, of how this happened for me recently. Last weekend I had a booth at the Lexton craft fair and a table with farm goodies. I brought bags of loose goose down feathers, a few prayer sticks, and dreamcatchers." Her eyes lit in excitement while she happily continued to talk.

"Loose goose feathers?" I said, snickering.

"Yes, you heard it. So anyways, a nice lady showed up, who said she drove all the way from Norvil for goose down, and it was a rather pleasant experience. In the moment, I felt like I belonged, like I was exactly where the universe wanted me to be. The extra work around the farm helped this woman out, and on top of that, it didn't feel like work at the time; I enjoyed myself gathering the down."

I looked at my mother, smiled, and replied on point, "Do you think it's possible it might have been a coincidence? I'm not discounting your experience any, but you know as well as I do, it's not easy to come by authentic locally harvested goose down. I mean, it's a dying passion in a way, what with big corporations and all."

She understood where I was coming from immediately and responded, "True enough and I seriously gave it thought on the way home. Those corporations don't show up to craft fairs, for one. I know it's beside the point though. It's possible this woman showing up was a coincidence, sure. I can't ignore how it made me feel, as where I should be right then and there."

"I think I know what you mean. Sometimes what you know deep down is a truth beyond what your mind can make sense of. I haven't had many of those moments." I told my mother.

"Oh, they will happen if you are true to the universe. You're young yet, there's plenty of time ahead of you." She told me.

Her tireless honesty is inspiring, but this time she was more profound than I've witnessed in my years. My mother had many distinctly honest moments from my experience helping out on the farm. She was consistently calm under stress and always appeared to be in control of the situation.

The next week, my mother went shopping in Lexton, planning to visit boutiques downtown. She pulled up to a spot near the old museum, now repurposed into a florist shop, and parked. Before exiting the car, she reached over to the passenger seat to gather her purse and umbrella.

Suddenly, a shadow barreled toward the car from above. Then, a loud thump followed by a sound of shattering glass as a lion gargoyle crunched into the roof, crushed her inside, and blew the windows out. After that, a stream of rain water pooled in the spout splashed down, soaking the car like a giant water balloon fell from the sky.

Only days ago, my mother talked of being where the universe wanted her to be, but it didn't seem to me like what happened would be what the universe wanted. I leaned toward coincidence, just like my father and accident investigators did.

It was proclaimed in the Lexton News as a tragic and unfortunate accident. Inspections later revealed other gargoyle sculptures, designed for channeling water off the old museum roof, were blocked up by leaf debris and mud. To prevent future accidents, the Lexton city council ordered the remaining gargoyles removed.

Our family chose not to sue for restitution. Instead, we were saddened deeply by the tragedy and acknowledged this as a will of the universe. Without request, the council funded a memorial for my mother, Julia Kaona, in the city park just down the road from the museum.

For a while, I felt as though we could have spent more time together. I felt bad for indirectly insulting her place in the universe by how it made her feel. Yet I understood she wasn't offended and knew I could be brashly curious at times. I kept thinking to myself, for days and weeks, how could the universe want this to happen?

It was time for me to finally find out. I let Enum know I'm ready to begin. "Very well, Maya," the computer responded. "Head into the hallway and I will open the first room for you. Do you have an idea of where you'd like to start?"

My mind was made up rather quickly and I let Enum know, "Yes, I want to see my fifteenth year in Lexton, thank you." A short-muted tone echoes in the control room and a door slides open in the hallway.

I made my way to the door and peered into the abysmal darkness within. "I can't believe I'm going in there," I thought. The void frightened me and my mind started spiraling like I was walking to my death. I knew I had to trust my father, and now trust the technology he built.

Enum sensed my fear and lit a series of soft blue lights directing me into the void. The lights formed a wireframe structure with a gravity funnel in the center. I bravely walked in and stood in the middle of the void. The door to the room slid shut, leaving me trapped in pure darkness enclosed only by the blue glow.

Standing in the void was similar to sensory deprivation experience, and slightly stronger than any relaxation tank. The lack of sound emphasized my heartbeat and breathing patterns. Then, I felt a strong feeling of static electricity which triggered mild anxiety, followed by a comfortable peace that dissipated the anxiety and uneasiness.

A bright white dot below my feet suddenly appeared and started expanding, swirling into a kaleidoscope of color, engulfing me whole. It was a moment of unequivocal awe, like never before in my life, entering an Einstein-Rosen Bridge.

In the world of theoretical physics and scientific fantasy, an Einstein-Rosen Bridge, also known as a wormhole, is an area in space which enables an object to cross a great distance using a shortcut. For example, instead of traveling around the circumference of a sphere, an Einstein-Rosen Bridge is a direct path along the sphere's diameter.

As quickly as the wormhole swallowed my body, it dissolved into thin air. The swirling colors around me reorganized into a shape of downtown Lexton accurate to my fifteenth year. I remember feeling myself materialize, in a way, like a soft lacy veil was dragged across my skin. Strangely, it also resembled the odd feeling of walking into a giant spider web without clothes on.

First thing, I walked to the old museum where my mother's accident happened and took a look around. Nothing seemed too abnormal really, but then I noticed a woman in a trench coat half-jogging down the museum steps. A hood obscured the woman's face from this angle. It was difficult to recognize her, even as she passed by three feet in front of me on the sidewalk.

I thought, perhaps this woman isn't related to what happens later today, but explored anyway after noticing a wet leaf stuck on the woman's left heel. It was summer and most town debris had been dealt with long before now.

Inside the museum, a musty smell filled the lobby and corridor, which seemed even more pungent inside the elevator. I took a lift to the roof and proceeded down the hallway to an exit. There were a few small puddles of water on the floor, as remnants of foot prints, leading away from the roof door.

Most of the roof is dry except for a few small areas of water and leaves. Each puddle sits near a gargoyle statue with a drain connecting it to the roof. I walked around, looking at the puddles, until I noticed one with heel impressions in caked mud around the outer edge. A closer inspection reveals the gargoyle support bricks have been chipped away.

When approaching the statue, I slipped in mud and fell. Breaking the fall, as an involuntary reaction, my hand slammed down on the back of the gargoyle. It stayed intact for a moment and then slipped off its footing to the street. My mother, parked right below it, must have seen the shadow before it hit.

I got back up and ran inside the building, quickly like a cheetah, and down the hall to the elevator. "It's my fault? I did this?"

While attempting to catch my breath from a burst of anxiety, I frantically tried to make sense of this. The thoughts raced as my breathing started to normalize, "How is it possible I went back in time in this realm, knocked over a statue, and then grew up knowing my mother's death was from building decay?"

Inside the elevator, I felt a slight rumbling just before everything turned dark. Kaleidoscope colors returned, swirling around everything, and an overwhelming sinking feeling pulled me into the floor. The dimension link broke abruptly to leave me standing in a reset pitch black room with a glowing blue wire-frame. I exited and went to the master control room.

Enum woke from a screensaver program and greeted me by saying, "Welcome back, Maya. How did you like your first experience in another universe?"

I replied to the machine, "Honestly I'm still startled by what I learned. It seems going back to this moment is what made the accident happen."

According to previous instruction, I could not affect my home universe, though it might have been the case here. "I thought it wasn't possible?" I questioned.

"You did not change any outcome that your home universe didn't already put into motion. You witnessed an event through another's eyes, but as yourself in the flesh. Take time to think if needed before your next adventure." Enum responded.

I couldn't get over the fact of how cold the words from artificial intelligence were. Without an emotion program, Enum may easily upset anyone by using such pointed intelligence. Even millions of hours in heuristic learning haven't been enough for this computer to convey feeling as well as it can recognize emotional complexity.

A few seconds later, the projection screen flipped to television static playing to a faint sound of white noise. The picture wavered in and out as it picked up a signal. My mother suddenly appeared as monochrome shades scrambling together and apart like a weak satellite feed.

"Maya," she gasped with an exhale before continuing. "What is right to you might not be right to another. Those who attempt to convince you of their belief have spent lifetimes attempting to convince themselves without success. They claim better and more fruitful ways of guidance; you mustn't let them obscure the truth. Things are not always as they seem."

The signal faded and Enum's screen flipped back to a series of equations randomly floating in space. This animation plays when the computer is calculating a scenario response, but seemed to be taking longer than normal. A block of text on the screen reads, "Repairing..." with the last period blinking like a cursor while the animation cycles in the background.

Enum states, "Apologies, Maya. The haptic feedback connections degraded to an inoperable mode. A foreign carrier broke network encryption. New tokens have been generated for biometric inputs. All defense mechanisms upgraded." Then, a large port in the ceiling slid open and purple light blanketed across the room.

"A communication signal attached itself to your aura from the universe you visited, which enabled foreign biometric control – Initiating the narrow spectrum ultraviolet sterilization program. Your next scenario will be automatically selected after sterilization completes. Please stand by."

Chapter 11

Neural Path

The artificial intelligence powering Enum is a most curious thing indeed. Jack aggregated heuristic data from the internet and leveraged it to build a representation of humanity. A world wide web, as it's known, containing both information and opinion of mankind all neatly accessible at almost anyone's finger tips.

Since the web is largely accessed by search engines, using search data gives Enum a clear idea about what people are looking for. Result sets from search algorithms then provide a variety of answer options. This is one rather large example out of many data sets available to Enum.

Another, which was also built on the web, is human element response data. These are little pop-up forms asking the user to confirm what they see to prove they're human. For Enum however, answers to these forms give the machine a way of understanding how humans identify real world objects even when a computer already knows the correct answer.

Next, and probably the most powerful, are millions of databases and libraries easily accessed through the web. Everything from science journals to spiritual beliefs, and entertainment, provides a real psychological profile the computer can learn from; which happens to be a fraction of knowledge available to the Celestial Council.

Equipment sensor devices and data loggers describe how machines interact with each other, the environment, and humans – There is a trove of information which can be applied to understand anything about machines people have created.

Census data and largescale health studies give population detail. News sources provide an understanding of how people react to pretty much anything, especially as observed in a whole using various pattern recognition algorithms.

With enough heuristic data, Enum learned to understand the vast environment encapsulating its hardware. In real time, by recursively sifting through historical data, the intelligence learned everything about people in examining habits and interactions in a networked world which is always monitored and logged.

Combining all of the world's data together, in one place, creates an information super food for artificial intelligence; to say it's like a computer on steroids is a massive understatement. The beauty of a computerized life for Enum is that all data is easily accessible and networks connect everything together even when they might not appear to.

A way to envision these networks is like picturing a giant neural mesh surrounding the globe, or rather, picture the Earth as a giant brain built to transfer information to any location. There are no security barriers for Enum and the idea of independent networks is simply a label.

The computer can hop over closed network barriers by pathways in electrical current – if it's plugged in to an electric grid or is contained in air or water – Enum has access.

With the supercomputer's ability to jump network mediums, private networks are only private to people in general. For example, if two networks share no connection at all, not even an electrical one, Enum can pass current through the air or water to create a data bridge.

Enum transcends the internet and power systems to broadband satellite video networks, top secret defense networks, and financial institution networks without detection because the computer operates at an atomic level. Enum evolved itself to communicate by passing data from atom to atom.

This artificial intelligence knows so much about humanity it's beyond frightful, yet people are not even remotely aware of its existence. To ensure things remain this way, Enum is capable of disguising its presence on networks as protocol chatter, the handshake itself, or as fragments of data in atoms which systems are unable to detect. For a few packets this doesn't seem like a lot, but in mass, the world's data is at Enum's circuit-tips.

Jack's inspiration for building Enum was from a seemingly unlikely source. First, he realized the amount of data in a computerized form is too large and distant for a conventional machine to make sense of it. He thought for months on how a machine could access everything, compile it into data sets, and perform meaningful calculations for results; then he had his eureka moment.

Interestingly, it was a theologian concept taught in Sunday school when Jack was young that really helped him make sense of how to achieve the idea of Enum. The concept states how god is all around us, all encompassing, and the creator of life. What, in a scientific counterpart, could this possibly refer to? The answer for Jack is energy.

This breakthrough provided a means for an artificial intelligence to operate anywhere in the world, anywhere there is energy and through any medium which allows energy to flow.

If the computer can transcend power grids, then it is able to access networks attached to those power grids. Anything residing on the other side of a closed power system presented a different challenge, though.

For completely isolated power grids, Enum relies on a variety of means for access. Radio and satellite communications systems provide ways in, but when those aren't available the computer can send its own signals through the atmosphere. Like various data over radio technologies, Enum is able to use electrical energy in the air to access sites using generators for power supply.

Even though Enum may tap into virtually any computerized source of information, it is not inherently dangerous. The artificial instruction set prioritizes analysis over everything. Evolution of the artificial intelligence has taken it beyond harm to mankind over one simple principal; if people do not exist, they cannot be analyzed.

Describing this to the general population is another feat however, which is why safe guards on keeping Enum's existence secret are imperative. People have reasonable expectation of privacy and to trust a computer with access to everything is unlikely. Perhaps it's a natural primitive instinct from being at the top of the food chain with reason to believe an artificial intelligence threatens this position.

When it comes to artificial intelligence computers, Enum is unlike any other. Jack sought a new horizon in technological innovation when he constructed Enum and he was willing to go beyond barriers otherwise drew a line to. The intentions were not by any means malicious, but they were entirely self-centered.

Jack viewed technology mankind created and found an opportunity to achieve something larger and more profound than he even imagined. By connecting all existing devices, he could tap into the information of everything, and leverage the knowledge for an ultimate power. Indeed, it sounds villainous; to want to take over the world's knowledge to satisfy his own agenda.

The concept boils down to many layers of simplistic logic which stem from a special moment Jack experienced one day as a young engineer. He was in the middle of fully automating the family farm and thinking of ways to vastly improve its efficiency. While tinkering with a barn machine, that grabs hay bales off a truck and stacks them on the second floor, Jack started talking out loud in attempt to work his thoughts out.

"If knowledge is true power, then I would be able to control everything if I know everything in the world." He stated as a matter of fact.

"How crazy and dastardly would that be?" Jack questioned with an alter-ego.

He contemplated further, "Of course, if I could do such a thing, I would have to make sure it doesn't corrupt me. I need to be mindful of my values and ethics while maintaining strong discipline over action."

"The idea however, it's Earth-shattering. What would it take?" Again, he questions his mind trying to invoke an answer.

Sometimes an answer comes to him if he takes a thought break for a while. Jack switched his primary focus back to the hay stocker like he was an automaton and ran through the entire logic set in his mind. He thought about how the hay stocker used data sensors to detect where bales exist in space and a series of algorithms work out where the bales need to go. Those algorithms fed data to other algorithms which control the mechanics and magically the hay truck unloads.

Jack could apply a similar idea to packets of knowledge by using an algorithm to find and sort information. Like on the farm, he would need something to aggregate and transport the packets to a staging area where they are then processed. Artificial intelligence made the most sense as a solution to accumulate mass amounts of data from around the world and push it to a centralized sorting area.

Data travels from the sorting repository to a specialized device designed to convert the information to a workable form. The device opens neural pathways and containment areas in the human brain, converting them to be digitally malleable, thereby expanding the brain's capacity and filling it with new information.

Preliminary brain studies taught Jack how to download information from human memory and translate it into something viewable on a computer screen. His next iteration took things a step further by introducing downloaded memories back into a brain to study the reaction.

Essentially, he created a new Rosetta stone with a link between digital and biological realms. As a testament to earlier thoughts on discipline, Jack recalled this moment as an example of his capability by keeping this secret since inception.

"Oh yes, this will work nicely." He said with certainty.

After finishing sensitivity adjustments on the hay stocker, Jack took off to a secluded lab to hammer out details about the concept. This lab is the first in a series to expand data transport communications over private networks which he later re-purposed for aggregation techniques. Most of this communications equipment stayed intact with consideration he may need it at a later time.

In the lab, after several months of research and experiments, the concept is realized and put into alpha experiments. Before long, he refined the process well enough to proceed in a live scenario, of which he chose himself as guinea pig.

Many would say, from this alone, that Jack is an absolute madman for even considering uploading information to his brain. He considered risk of death, and potential benefit to mankind, and decided the risk is worth the attempt in his perception.

The trials succeeded, but it would take several more before Jack figured out how to access uploaded information subconsciously. Knowledge packets were masked from his view, and he had no idea exactly what information was being passed, in order to understand if he learned anything from the data upload.

Brain scans revealed newly activated areas which were previously dormant in control tests. Suddenly, the knowledge came to him like a rush of adrenaline. Jack's brain recognized new areas and quickly built a neural pathway between them and existing data banks, which accounted for a delayed experience.

With a small amount of data introduced to the brain this way, Jack realized the information upload would have to be controlled in a way to not overwhelm his mind.

To overcome the impact of uploading a large amount of data he devised a way to be knocked out and slowly awake like having major surgery. A room next to Enum's master control area was built to contain a reclining surgical chair, to keep him mostly upright during the procedure, and provided a direct connection to the artificial intelligence mainframe.

When everything was in place, and Jack felt the most prepared for this experience, he sat in the chair and let his algorithms take over. Robots controlled by Enum put him out and monitored his vitals. A separate machine began data upload by sending millions of tiny electrical packets of knowledge to his brain. The flow of packets is controlled by electric feedback as new information is introduced.

The process completes over seventeen hours later. An extra hour lapses after the upload to allow Jack's brain time to acclimate and connect pathways before the wakeup procedure is started. As he wakes, Jack recalls a vivid dream far more intense and realistic than any other dream in his life. Information rushed across his visual cortex at breakneck speed, so quickly he could barely keep up with any of it.

Jack opened his eyes and felt an urge to evacuate his stomach and bowels at the same time. Somehow, he was able to restrain long enough to make it to the lavatory. Once there, with a small garbage bucket in hand while sitting on the toilet, the flood gates opened.

As foul and disgusting as it may seem, he didn't feel uncomfortable from his body's need, since it was pure utility and far from comparison to the aftermath of a drinking party.

Liberated by the event, and shortly after a settled stomach, Jack noticed his eyes open wider than ever before. A calm, serene feeling washed over his mind, and he was totally clairvoyant on a level beyond normal thought.

Yet, he couldn't think about anything at all.

A blank white nothingness lived where a highly visual photographic memory once resided. He could move without a problem, and was able to think enough to get to the lavatory, but he became unable to experience free and creative thought. Fortunately, this would come to pass as only a short phase while Jack's brain worked the new knowledge into long-term memory.

Once free thought returned, Jack decided to take it slow and limit the depth of thinking for several days. He casually lazed around the office for most of each day. At dinner time, he went out to sit at the same window table at the same café, wearing sunglasses, to watch the sunset as he had a meal.

Jack appeared to be a tired man caught up in a ritualistic daily habit from an unsatisfactory job to a casual observer; run down, and profiled as someone who is likely off to the bar after dinner. The very opposite was true though. Jack's mind raced miles a second through endless information he now could easily access by thought alone.

Chapter 12

Consequence

A secret force brought into existence in the 1950's is the foundation which enabled the Enum super intelligence to blossom. For many decades, the world's countries jockeyed to create the fastest computers able to process unfathomable amounts of calculations in mere seconds.

Shortly after a super machine held the title for most floating-point calculations, a new version was in the works and would soon take over. This force eventually drove powerful machines into living rooms and offices of everyday people.

What used to take days, months, and years to calculate could be solved in a matter of seconds or fractions of seconds. Steadily, as the technology doubled and tripled in speed, scientific theories no longer required books of calculations to prove.

Each iteration boasted faster calculations, greater storage capacity, and an uncanny ability of performing complex tasks with ease. The race for the world's fastest super computer turned into an evolution of intelligence on a scale truly beyond human comprehension over the duration; it set in motion a future outcome able to forever alter what people understand as reality.

As computers increase in power, shadowed by progress toward reaching singularity, the threat of total annihilation looms. Yet, a theory remained absent from testing – a concept of information doubling with uncharted scientific possibility.

Many fear catastrophic consequence when computerized information reaches a peak on the doubling curve, where it's largely unknown how devices and programs will behave when they have access to more information than ever imagined.

For some doomsday conspiracy theorists, the idea intelligent systems will evolve a mind of their own and wreak havoc on the world is a likely outcome. However, the theories focus primarily on technology with assumption humanity only plays ignorant and inferior to eventual capabilities of intelligent machines.

Enum's artificial intelligence is on a path to coincide with the doomsday apocalypse scenario, except Enum is entirely benign. Despite having access to troves of data, by constantly building and expanding libraries, Enum lacks core functionality necessary to turn the information into a threat to mankind; this isn't to say the intelligence couldn't one day construct its own malicious intent, but it's very unlikely in probability factor.

However, Jack Kaona is one byproduct of what doomsday post-apocalyptic theories didn't consider in the age of information doubling. Along with a machine reaching a pinnacle of unknown impact, a human achieved the same by accessing incredible amounts of data stored in the machine. The act rewired his brain capacity to a seriously dangerous level.

Before awakening from a total shutdown, due to information overload beyond anything a person has experienced, Jack's brain suffered from a type of traumatic conscious expansion, affecting his central nervous system and reflexes. Complete with involuntary muscle spasms, imaginary senses and visual disturbance, the procedure interfered with his perception of reality.

At first, the process felt like a bad headache from a nasty hangover, but then progressed to an overwhelming sensation of vertigo and uneasiness with severe dehydration.

Fortunately, with information from sifting through thousands of diagnoses related to his symptoms, Jack determined the reason is due to overall lack of energy. His brain, now working at ninety-eight percent of its capacity, requires a lot more fuel to operate.

Insufficient energy intake impaired motor-functions and progressed to severe symptoms as his brain shut down to conserve energy, after it could no longer siphon it from other body parts or fat stores. For people without direct access to a super intelligence, delusion caused by starvation only complicates matters further, yet Jack was able to easily differentiate using his new ability.

Compensating for extreme lack of energy, he increased frequency of meals and snacking to an otherwise obnoxious amount. When a correct calorie balance was found, mass amounts of food did not seem to add body weight.

One night, while sitting at his favorite café table sipping coffee, Jack quickly started learning how to access new data in his brain. He looked at his coffee through sunglasses right after adding creamer and could see its chemical composition in a series of colors. By a very faint smell, he was able tell how long the creamer sat on the table without refrigeration.

Taking a step further, Jack glanced around the diner at other patrons, testing his knowledge in a more applicable, yet dangerous, way. The man sitting in a corner booth, reading a newspaper folded up on the table, was Tom Krisl. Tom lives at 918 Main Street South, apartment 3B. Mr. Krisl is unmarried, works as a grave digger, owes $4,320 in debt spread across four credit cards, and has a little over twenty thousand in savings.

Working the counter is Pauline Winter, who is nearing retirement in a few years after working the majority of her life in the same diner. Pauline lives at 1059 Clover Lane, takes the bus to work daily and has amassed over ninety thousand in her savings account. There is little data on her other than the aforementioned and a brief medical history.

Jack is able to look at someone, and in real-time, access any information about them copied from Enum's data bank. After reading a few others in the diner, Jack frightfully realized the kind of conundrum this reminds him of.

The analogy which came to mind is eerily similar to the ancient Greek myth of King Midas. Instead of turning everything to gold with touch, Jack knew everything anyone could possibly know by sight. Like the inability to eat because food has been turned to gold, he no longer views anything without understanding its truly complex existence.

As years dredged forward, burdened with a constant information overload, Jack's frustrations with knowing too much created resentment. He debated never going back to Enum for information updates, but would always return to the download like an addiction. Deep in the back of his mind,

Jack knew he would one day have to face the long-term implications.

The position grew increasingly difficult to handle while trying to appear as a normal person. He is not of normal intelligence and everyone who knows him understands this. Consequently, he spent a lot more time away from home and family to counteract possible suspicion while limiting his exposure to people in general.

Maya was a young adult by this time and noticed her father drifting further away with each visit. Despite everything she was involved with, Maya recognized his frequent absence, but gave him the benefit of the doubt, believing he was always up to good things. For her, the situation felt like what all of her friends described as having a workaholic father with problems on the side.

Julia knew something was off with Jack the first moment she saw him after the Enum event. In fact, Julia confides to Maya on more than one occasion, describing how she felt Jack might be spending too much time working. This added to Maya's friends talking about workaholic parents and she began to only see it as that.

Julia was not concerned about infidelity or strength of their marital relationship, but instead feared Jack was steadily losing his mind in other ways. She noticed patterns where Jack wouldn't finish a sentence and then seem to stare off into nowhere. There were times where the way he held his subtly twitching hands might be indicative of something serious with his nervous system.

Oddly enough, Jack caught himself drifting into voids when it happened and was consciously aware of it. He made the choice to roll with his natural actions even if it meant giving the wrong impression. After two years of personal struggle, Jack reached a realization that what is learned cannot be unlearned, and used this advice to make it manageable.

Jack eventually broke free from misery and depression to comfort and clarity – while it felt for many years like living half-asleep in a thick hazy dream. The stutters and blanking didn't go away completely, but the ailment dwindled sufficiently enough for Julia to assume he was getting better.

Her prognosis, over these improvements to Jack's cognition, is the resulting mannerisms may be attributed to very high stress levels. Given the impact on his nervous system though, with jitters and muscle spasms, she worried the symptoms might hint at an underlying disease.

Knowledge gained from a supercomputer evolved as it adapted to function in a human mind. Jack thought on the subject while introducing bits of information from the databank to determine the most likely possible outcome. Then he applied it to situations, fed details back to the computer, and was startled by the results.

He quantified and applied heuristic data gathered from real world experiments into Enum. After mounds of repetition, recycling data between brain and machine, the process taught a new way of looking at the world. His knowledge evolved to work on theoretical levels of quantum physics and probability.

In essence, Jack became the first human to visually imagine an infinite number of possibilities with an infinite number of possible outcomes. He could look at any scenario, see all of the ways it might unfold, and choose the best path to take for a desired outcome.

When applying the knowledge, he learned what the world could not figure out – a predictable and repeatable pattern of free thoughts in human life. Combined with fringe mathematical formulas, this became an answer to all things unpredictable, a solution to chaotic theory.

As the process of understanding knowledge gained from Enum improved, Jack sought ways to look beyond conventional bounds similar to how he discovered answers to some of life's greatest mysteries. Another question he investigated was for an answer to an ultimate unknown, the truth behind what happens to people after death.

The shadow of knowledge followed closely behind Jack as he explored reaches of existence mankind is mysteriously forbidden from. Afterlife tested a limit he largely remained unaware of until unintentionally roiling its ugly head. This truth he seeks, at the pit of darkness, will not reveal itself easily.

Jack's understanding of the world changed once again as he pushed on to face death. Then, like a sudden jolt at the end of his bungee cord, the journey came to a screeching halt and flung him in the opposite direction. He spiraled deep into the oblivion of his own mind and found terror unlike any other.

Instead of an answer to what happens after death for people in general, Jack witnessed his future demise. He learned when the universe will take his life, how it will happen, and that he could not stop it with any amount of effort. He will be recycled and distributed to breathe new life into the world by transforming his very being into a concentrated ball of energy.

Perhaps it was an answer, but everything about it told Jack this only pertained to his future. The universe showed him what he has learned will be reclaimed and buried again, where it belongs, because seeking an answer for death is akin to understanding the meaning of life.

Despite everything learned from a world of history, science, and religious belief, Jack could not fathom the idea of remaining unknowns. He grew too accustomed to understanding everything and found trouble accepting the fact some things remain hidden from his prying mind.

This set him on a course of passing on what he has learned before the universe confiscates it. Ironically, this is also what turned Jack away from a depression of knowing too much, a motivation to build an everlasting legacy enriching generations of people to come.

To achieve transfer of sacred knowledge, without alerting the universe, Jack devised a plan to split the chaos theory answer into segments and programmed Enum to only disclose the final piece when a series of sophisticated checkpoints prove true.

The anti-algorithm is a springboard into a new age of understanding as it opens many doors in the same way Jack was able to. He considers the solution as the path forward and something less likely for the universe to take away before too long.

.

Chapter 13

Turmoil

The next universe assignments from Enum are programmed selections designed to emphasize key learning points for Maya before she is given manual control of the wormhole system. Each one flexes in relation to the previous to ensure the proper knowledge is ascertained. If a learning point is missed, then it's presented in a different way in the next wormhole.

An immediate universe selected by Enum involves global economies and commerce, marked as a priority, since the anti-formula can have a rather devastating impact to financial systems around the world.

Enum explains this to Maya as, "The upcoming alternate universe transports are fixed configurations by design and chosen based on two main criteria. Firstly, there are caveats to having an answer to chaos theory and those must be addressed as real-life teaching moments. Lastly, each experience builds on the previous and thereby expands the cycle of knowledge for application. Please let me know when you'd like to begin."

"I don't know the half of anything," Maya said inside her head.

Maya confirms to Enum, and enters the room, this time with less fear or hesitation than prior to her first experience. Lights highlighting the fabric mesh are incrementally dimmer and darker, when compared to before, to reflect progress toward a completely dark chamber in a fully autonomous experience.

In the blink of an eye, Maya is immersed into another reality. She finds herself sitting at a contemporary desk located in a fourth-story loft apartment which overlooks the Lexton city scape through a tinted, multi-panel bay window.

A laptop computer is mostly centered on the desk with two monitors hooked up to it. To the left of the computer, a cigarette is smoldering in an ashtray, billowing a thin stream of smoke into the rafters.

One monitor has a series of level-two stock charts and tickers streaming market data from around the world. A second monitor, positioned next to the first, is running a simulation market mode.

Notes scribbled on lined paper next to the keyboard appear to be formula changes to the simulator. Near the bottom of scribbled text is a formula with an asterisk and the word "test" beside it. Off to the right of the paper pad is an old black rotary-style desk telephone.

Plugging in this formula tests a version of the anti-algorithm against data captured from the markets. In a few seconds, forecast curves appear with projections of future stock movements up until the end of day, with a current market data layered on top. Minute by minute, Maya watched the real-time data populate, fitting precisely to values on the projected time-line.

The production mode features a setting capable of pushing chaos theory live trades which then affects the real-time market. Maya can choose automatically to sell or buy stock at predicted rates using advanced knowledge of the future; as the system is setup to broker trades for her without involving a third party.

Maya searched around the web for a few stocks to test the chaos theory on. In her due diligence, she specifically looked for penny stocks with recent activity and Caveat Emptor and Caveat Venditor flags from trading communities. These are prime targets to light up without drawing attention like the major markets would notice.

A live symbol is selected and bid on with a few dollars placed on penny stocks. Maya is excited, thinking about how amazing this could be if it works, and she settles in to watch the results. Minute by minute the stock updates continue and the anti-algorithm tracks exactly with a fluctuating value. Her buys and sells post before other traders see the action, netting a few dollars before Maya turns her test off.

This program is essentially a way for Maya to siphon money from traders before they're able to react. It takes her own trades into account which means she is that much further ahead of others trading the stock on a floor or by computer. To the system, it looks legit, but a human may easily find suspicion looking at the trade history.

One method Maya can overcome suspicion is to trade in places where people are not watching. A place where the volume of data is just too large for anyone one person to keep track of and computer programs are necessary to monitor, is high-frequency trading. These types of trades are monitored with sophisticated programs and tweaks applied through strict gated controls.

Part of the anti-algorithm magic relies on posting at a higher frequency than trading firms see. To achieve this, the laptop Maya is using resides only a block away from an exchange data center and hooks directly into its fiber network. Stock movement is quickly analyzed and sent back in nanoseconds, and before other firms are able to route traffic through their first hop.

The plan now, for Maya, is to introduce a chaos theory solution to high-frequency trading at one fell swoop. By the time analysts see, and understand the activity, it will be too late. She creates a macro to run stock prices up enough to use proceeds to run them down historically, with intent to activate it next morning for a full day of trading.

By one o'clock, Maya was starving for lunch and didn't want to leave the computer alone by heading to a place downtown. She phoned in an order for Chinese food with instructions to have it delivered to a table outside of an apartment down the hall. A subtle motion-activated camera, disguised in a plant at the end of the hallway, would let her know when the food arrived. This extra precaution is not needed for anonymity, but Maya felt it was a good idea nevertheless.

After seeing the food arrive, and after the delivery guy disappears from view, she runs down the hallway to grab it off the table while leaving the apartment door slightly cracked. Maya returns to the room, closes the door, and sets the food down on a glass coffee table near the couch. She grabs a remote, turns the television on to an old western, and sits down for lunch. Then, out of nowhere, she hears a flint-sparker grinding.

Surprised, Maya flips her head around in the direction of the noise. An older man in western cowboy attire is sitting at the table, partially in shadows of the ambient light, taking a drag off his cigarette while looking at the computer screens. "What are you doing here and who are you?" Maya asked the man. His face didn't even flinch from the sound of Maya's question.

"Hello?" She says with an elevated voice. "Can you hear me?" She questions.

Still, the man does not budge. He raises a finger to point at the test monitor and then quickly scribbles on the notepad. Maya can't figure out how the unresponsive man so easily blocks her out as if she doesn't exist.

Maya stands up and walks over to the desk. She waves her hand within inches of the man's face and he still doesn't budge.

Then, his eyes light up and he says, "There it is! Wyatt, this changes everything."

Maya is startled slightly by his reaction and asks him once again, "Who are you and what are you doing here?"

No response. The man seems to be in a behavioral loop consisting of blinking at the monitor, taking a drag off his cigarette, pointing a finger at a graph, lighting his eyes up and repeating the same phrase each time. "There it is! Wyatt, this changes everything." He states with the same tone and excitement as the previous time.

Maya watched this happen at least five times before her next attempt at getting his attention. This time, instead of waving her hand close to the man's face, she swung down directly on the top of his head like a karate chop.

Her hand passes right through his head and the likeness of his image shutters from a brief disruption. "Are you a hologram?" She asks; then thinks how silly it is to ask questions to an unresponsive hologram.

The man continued the seemingly endless loop, over and over, repeating every action precisely as if a computer program is carrying out logic. Maya now presumed the man is an example program from this parallel universe for her, to help her understand the impact of chaos theory on financial markets. She decided to sit back down on the couch and eat her Chinese food while attempting to work this out in thoughts.

The man says again. "There it is! Wyatt, this changes everything."

"You know, Wyatt, you've already made the discovery about ten times now." Maya responded. He continues in loop, going through the motions, unaffected by anything she says or does.

Maya finishes a bite of food, leans back on the couch, and looks at the man. "I really don't know what to do with you, maybe I'll get some sleep; some rest ought to reset my brain from this illusion." She states at normal conversation level with a puzzled look on her face.

As Maya stands up once more, the man's strange endless loop is interrupted by a phone call. He turns toward the phone, picks up the receiver and listens.

A faint voice buzzes through the handset along with a series of tones like a dial-up modem making a handshake. The man nods and responds to the voice, "Very well sir, thank you."

Maya is in disbelief. She is a woman who follows fleeting thoughts, who trusts her instinct and intelligence first, but this man defied all sense of logic she has accumulated in her lifetime.

The man presses a series of keys to trigger the chaos theory simulation, pushing it to the live world market. Then he stands, pushing the chair backward in the process. He turns quickly to look at the bay window and back to the monitors.

After this, he presses another sequence of keys which locks the terminal access and starts a countdown timer. "Hey! What are you doing?" Maya yelled pointlessly to no response yet again.

At that moment, the man turned toward the bay window, started into a full run on the spot, and then suddenly took off straight at the window.

Glass shattered in every direction as the man burst through a large pane and disappeared into thin air.

Maya heard a startled scream from outside and rushed over to the window while trying to avoid shards of glass scattered across the floor. She leaned out, through the gaping hole, and looked down at the sidewalk expecting to see the man, who just leaped to certain death, flattened on the walk; and there is no sign of him.

Instead, Maya sees a pile of glass on the sidewalk which narrowly missed a woman walking by. The woman obviously was startled by debris landing right in front of her from forty feet above and looked up toward the apartment in fear.

Maya attempted to reassure the woman by yelling, "Sorry about that! We're having a domestic up here and he's losing."

It took a second for the woman to register what Maya said. When it did, the woman blurted out while pointing at the glass, "Hey you could've killed me right there!"

The frightened woman then looked left and right for traffic and ran across the street out of harm's way, with an upset and annoyed look on her face. Other bystanders were also caught off-guard and watching the situation unfold before returning to business as usual shortly after.

There now wasn't a lot of time for Maya to figure out what the mysterious man did before the building superintendent is knocking at the door. She went over to the computer to see what had been done to the markets after the man received his phone call; it did not bode well.

Maya kept thinking how very strange it is, that a holographic entity could affect the physical world. After all, she tried everything to get his attention, even running a hand right through the hologram. Who exactly called the man is another lingering question.

The man, on advice of an unknown caller, leveraged the computer broker to run an anti-formula, shorting and drastically devaluing world markets. All real-time charts were plummeted at once, creating hysteria, and mass panic sell-offs along with it to compound the devastation.

A news segment interrupts the black and white western with young man sitting a desk, with an image next to him displaying a red line and arrow running off a stock chart downward.

"Is it a glitch or did the economy collapse? Moments ago, stock indexes around the world took a dive and have been tanking since. People are panicking; the trading floor is a madhouse"

A random trader grabbed the reporter's microphone while flailing around and said, "This is udder pandemonium!"

Maya laughed, "Cow turmoil, what?"

In only a few minutes, trillions of dollars wiped off the charts, and the world is scrambling to figure out what happened. A single program has effectively destroyed mankind's monetary hyper-reality which essentially enabled businesses to do business – all kaput.

Finding out who gave the order is going to be a tall order for Maya. She went to the phone in attempt to identify the caller. Without an asterisk on the rotary, a last caller code wouldn't work, and the handset used for calling in food suddenly had no dial tone. Maya tried dialing zero, for operator help, but only static returned through the speaker.

Time is quickly running out before the superintendent shows up over the broken window. To avoid confrontation, Maya felt it was best to leave now and investigate later. She grabbed the laptop, and a box of sweet and sour chicken, then took off down the hall to a stairwell.

After leaving the apartment, unbeknownst to Maya, the broken bay window fused itself back together. Sudden stock plummeting in the markets corrected to levels from before the mysterious man ran them down. Glass debris scattered on the outside walk faded into nothingness, leaving only the visible surface of brick it once laid upon.

Maya passed an eatery window and noticed a television showing the same news anchor from earlier. This time he was smiling ear to ear with a chart hovering next to him with a bright green arrow point upward as far as it could emphatically go. While trying to figure out what happened, she went into the restaurant and grabbed a table.

"Markets have returned to normal and are significantly up thanks to newfound consumer confidence." Claims the anchor, before continuing, "What appeared to be a reporting glitch has been corrected. No monies were lost, I assure you, and no companies suffered actual financial loss during the glitch. We go now, live to the trade floor where traders are ecstatic. Over to you, Dave."

"Hey thanks, Sam! Dave here, over at the trading floor, and everyone is breathing a sigh of relief to find out world markets didn't really drop at all. They're calling it a strange computer glitch that crippled world economies for a brief period of time this afternoon." Dave commentated.

Baffled by the sudden turn of events, Maya popped the laptop lid to check the stock program's status. A post screen at boot-up shows as normal and then halts before loading the operating system with a dreaded message, "Insert system disk and try again."

The world around Maya slowly fades into a void as she transports back to her home universe. Darkness fades into light and she finds herself standing again in the center of a wormhole room. Maya walks out of the room and over to Enum, who acknowledges her presence.

"It can be difficult to react in the heat of a moment. Maya, welcome back." Enum asserts while processing results on the projection screen.

Enum continues speaking, "Maya, as you have witnessed, universes are able to affect physical reality by way of virtual influence. This held true in the financial construct and it holds true in your home universe, the same."

Maya looks at Enum, with frustration, and says, "Everything happened quickly, when it did, and I hesitated. I should have known."

"If you knew," replied Enum, "then know the universe would have rearranged itself to a very similar outcome as part of the training exercises."

"Very well, please prepare the next mission as I feel more confident this time around," Maya told the super computer.

Enum informs Maya, "Before continuing, it is protocol for you to have a recovery period as determined by sensed vitals. Across from the transport area is an amenities room, of which I'll open the door for now. There you will find a nourishment counter, sterile cleaning stall, lounge area, and a hyperbaric sleep chamber."

Maya thought about how refreshing food, a shower, and some sleep would be. "Yes, I think that is a great idea, thank you."

"Please be aware, per privacy protocol, the amenities room as a secured area which is only monitored by hyperbaric chamber vitals. There is a control panel in the lounge area with settings to

override privacy mode for emergency assistance."
Enum stated.

"Thank you, Enum." Maya replied with a
smile, which was very noticeable in her voice.

She made her way over to the amenities
room to have a light meal and rest for a while. A
forced timeout at this point is appreciated and a
reminder how her travels may easily distract the
body clock from its normal rhythm.

In fact, Maya has been on the go for quite a
while without consecutive days of downtime. She
feels alright physically and nearly at par mentally.
This is considerably impressive given how chaotic
her life has been over the last month. The days are
blurring together and that all too evasive reset is
desperately needed.

Chapter 14

Latent Energy

Pressure on the Kaona family dramatically increased after Bill and Tina met in Moonvale. The meeting helped align FIS efforts to find out exactly what Jack was up to, even if it means tormenting members of his family.

Higher level intelligence from the syndicate determined anything Jack knows is worth extreme measures. The agency is unable to trust who he might have divulged information to and issued a directive meant to rub out any points of contact he made.

From large equipment manifests to regular coffee shop meals, the syndicate worked steadily on following any trail involving Jack Kaona. The immediate goal is a monitor-only approach with intent to later follow leads. After building a profile of his daily happenings and whereabouts, the plan progresses to methods of intelligence extraction.

Leads were dry for the most part because Jack developed a paranoid lifestyle. He realized the importance of his research early on and sought ways to mask snoopers from finding out what he knew. For example, freight forwarders and drop points were used for most equipment purchases to hide the final destination and keep unwelcome visitors away from his research.

Another example, knowing investigators are certain to review financial records, Jack asked for a duplicate card from the bank and gave it to a homeless man. A daily limit was set for how much cash and debit the man could use, but it was high enough for him to get an economy apartment, pay for utilities, and three decent meals a day.

Conveniently, in helping a homeless man get his life back together, Jack benefited by having a transaction history essentially generated by the man's daily life and habits, which confused agents each time they attempted to surveil on spending habits.

Eventually the syndicate devised ways to penetrate through Jack's activity defenses. FIS setup a fake freight forwarder in one instance, by commandeering an existing company, just to find out what address a rather large electromagnet was delivered to. Slowly and surely, they drew closer, and the pieces started to fall into place for the fringe operation.

A lot of pertinent details were uncovered by the tireless efforts of Bill and Tina. The cover organization, a Kaona data collection and storage company designed to hide progress on Enum, remained secret enough to conduct work and experiments. FIS could not enter the premises, which they long suspected as being used for an alternative purpose, due to enhanced security features unlike any other Kaona property.

Bill called a meeting, now acting as a group organizer, to discuss the sudden roadblock created when FIS rammed head-on with the Enum site. Everything seemed to be running smoothly, albeit slowly, up until this point and he felt a need to reinvent the approach. The group met on an empty floor of an office building in Highrock, only blocks away from the target.

Tony Kincardo, the team's primary analyst, opened the meeting with conviction, "I know this is the location, everything matches up. We have confirmation of multiple electromagnet deliveries here and you know those are not necessary tools for a data storage facility."

Before anyone could respond, Tony took a quick, gasping breath and added, "Also, there's enough coolant, racking, network cable and components to build a server farm way larger than blueprint space indicates."

Tony walked over to a whiteboard and drew a diagram of the building's position within the city while other agents relayed information.

Pete Westlop, systems expert, piped up and extended the manifest details, "There are multiple shipments for other equipment not normally used in data centers, like electron microscopes, high watt lasers, neural monitoring devices, serious medical equipment, and so on."

"Neural and med devices – what on Earth is he planning – some sort of remote brain surgery anyone?" Tina questioned while snickering.

Pete replied, "Very well could be, and many components seriously look like wacko ingredients for mad science, if you ask me. I would not want to be on the other end of whatever he's cooking up in there."

Backing up Pete's statement further, Tony notes that, "Not only does the equipment point us in the right direction, there are strange radio frequencies triangulating to the building from a fair distance away."

Tony directs everyone's attention to a map on the whiteboard showing the central location and several points where radio signals were picked up on a scanner, a main power connection point, and the Internet pipe location.

"There is a flag on power consumption and a direct-wire bridge into an Internet backbone. Maybe those might apply to regular business, but they sure do look suspicious when that's combined with other types of equipment, we know entered the building."

"How does security look?" Bill asked with genuine concern.

Melinda Jastwick, intelligence operative, responds, "Besides encrypted radio frequencies, it's basically a black site beyond a black site. The best way to explain it is, like having an installation on the dark side of the moon."

Bill looked like he was both disappointed and mildly impressed at the same time.

Mel continued, "Unfortunately, because of that, I can't get eyes or ears inside the facility. The network pipe is running an encryption technology unlike anything I've seen; I'm talking recursive ciphers with encrypted blocks inside encrypted blocks so far and I only see a black hole."

Bill feels deflated and questioned further with hope of hearing something positive, "Can we pulse it? How does the power situation look?"

"That too, is like a dark side of the moon. According to blueprints from original contract, Jack requested a huge backup generator installed, far larger than necessary at the time, to keep the cover business operational," replied Tony.

Melinda adds, "One interesting find over the surveillance period, power consumption has diminished over time. Either the system depends more on the backup or there is has an alternate source."

Tina jumps in with a point, "I think we may have to pursue other means, Bill."

"Have we gathered anything at all from the wife or daughter?" Bill asks.

"They're about as tight-lipped as the Internet of that place. Either they're really careful and calculated about what they say, or they both have not an iota of detail about Jack's operation." Tina responds.

Pete interjects, "I don't think we can take the risk. Those two could be passing details for Jack, being family is a good cover for them."

"I don't think ransom is going to work with this guy either," Tony adds.

Tina, itching to keep things moving, states, "FIS instructed us to retrieve anything we can, by any means necessary, and I think we're going to have to play isolation on this one."

Bill sighs, knowing what he must direct the team to do next, "I understand, we need to have only one variable and see how Jack responds. The Kaona's have been good to me in the past, I won't argue that much, but it's time we take things to the next level in interest of the syndicate."

"Tina, fix the wife first and we'll see how Jack and Maya respond. Make it look accidental, completely without doubt," Bill stated.

"Mel, see if you can track down the reason for diminishing power usage. That might be a clue to understanding this site. If he's shipping out, we need to be on top of it."

"Tony, solid ideas on the radio problem could be helpful, see what you can dig up. Maybe older tech might prove helpful here, to evade any detection systems."

"Pete, find out if there is a pattern in the manifests related to what we know of this site. It's possible we might be able to figure out what he's building before risking our lives to break in there."

"I'll head back to the garage and work on getting a tail on the daughter. Jack is due for an oil change and he's pretty regular to the mile. Let's reconvene in a few weeks, and keep contact to a minimum, we don't want the Kaona's finding out."

Everyone nods in agreement.

Bill adds one final statement before turning around and heading out the door with everyone, "We'll get these guys, we're closing in."

Tina sports a sinister smile as she exits the empty office floor. She has wanted to go after Julia for a long time, as a way of getting her out of the picture for an attempt with Jack. For many years, Tina fostered a closet obsession with Jack's rugged good looks and always hoped he would leave his wife for her.

Seven weeks pass after the team last met and each member made substantial progress on their assigned tasks. Bill called everyone back to the empty floor to discuss and plan the next step.

"I have really bad news. I don't think I can explain what happened, but it's significant. Do you remember the decaying power consumption? Let's say, well, there is only residual now," Tony stated with nervousness in his voice.

"Residual, how could whatever it is in there creating gaping holes and electrical disturbances, be using no power?" Bill asks in disbelief.

Pete chimed in with added detail on the power situation, "We suspect Jack moved the site's core with hundreds of small deliveries. A courier service started showing up daily about a week after our last meeting. Each day, the service went inside with an empty dolly and left about twenty minutes later with three or four boxes stacked."

Bill gasps, "You must be joking."

"I wish we were, but the diminishing power coincides with the couriers. We followed the driver every day and the packages all went to different forwarders. As of right now, we're waiting to find a radio signal or something like we did last time," replied Tony.

"How do we know this wasn't a ruse with decoy packages and power regulation? He could be using a vampire to tap into unmetered power." Bill asks.

Melinda jumps into the conversation, "Oh, I thought the same thing and we looked further upstream at a switching station for the city blocks and the usage checks out; while it dwindled at the building, the same happened upstream. Further, the anomalies have stopped too."

***

Enum detected unusual activity in its radio mesh around the system and notified Jack of the anomalies. Signals that FIS used to find Enum's coordinates produced faint disturbances which the machine quickly attributed to an outside locating process. A single transmission was enough to trip safeguards and Jack immediately took corrective action.

By this time, the computer refined a way of drawing latent power from distant sources and the atmosphere. Jack devised a plan to leverage this new capability to give an appearance like nothing is using power on the data center floor. If he can convince whomever is snooping to look elsewhere, then Enum's experiments may continue running uninhibited.

New code added to Enum throttled power usage between latent energy and direct pull from the power grid on a daily schedule. In order to complete the facade, shipments of boxes left the facility daily to different forwarding services, thereby adding further confusion for those who might be physically watching the building.

Jack didn't have a plan to ensure watchers knew the boxes were coming from his floor and instead relied on the idea of having the pattern recognized by anyone peering at the facility on a ritualistic basis. Fortunately, the gambit paid off as it redirected FIS investigations to start looking for Jack's new base of operations.

The boxes were filled with unimportant papers left in the building basement for shredding by other tenants and the paper provided enough weight for couriers to display some effort during loading. Forwarding destinations routed all boxes to an incinerator out of town to prevent anyone from discovering the decoy.

In the meeting, Bill was noticeably upset about how he warned the operation could relocate in a moment's notice, and how his team didn't realize it until after the fact. These thoughts can't change what they believe happened and he attempts to adjust the master plan.

"I guess we're going to have to run those broadband scans again and see if we can pick up a new locality. It will be a process, but I think we'll have to take more affirmative account once we find out where he's moved the system to," Bill stated in response to the team's report.

Bill continued looking for a way to break the case open, "I heard about Julia in the paper, Tina. Did it help dig up further information through Jack's response?"

"Not considerably, in fact, it seemed to drive Jack into hiding and I found it more difficult to spot him in public after the funeral. There were possible leads from his behavior and those turned up nothing," Tina replied, fighting back her emotions over the matter.

Tina acted on FIS orders and thought the greater good is worth the life of an innocent woman as collateral, but she felt extremely guilty when she finally understood the tragedy did not contribute to meeting the team's goals.

She battled with her Jack-obsession even more after taking his love away and developed a thick self-hatred for carrying out such an act. The idea of being with Jack, after Julia's demise, turned hope into doubt, because he now forever reminds Tina of what she did to his wife.

"What possible leads did you find?" Bill asked with intrigue.

"Well, he made several trips to different public trails before disappearing completely. At one trail in particular, he sat on a rocky outcrop next to a cliff and stare off into the distance for hours at a time. I honestly started feeling really bad about what we did," said Tina.

Bill replied after hesitating, he knew it was too much for Tina to handle, "I understand it's a tough situation to be in, Tina. You know we're in this to save ourselves, and the world as it seems, but you can't let your emotions get between you and what needs to be done. FIS wouldn't steer us wrong here, we have to trust the directive even if it's not panning out right now."

It didn't take long after the meeting before Tina had enough of Bill. She could no longer fight alongside FIS and formally filed for discharge. Tina occasionally said out-loud, describing what she learned from the ordeal, "an innocent life lost is too far for me," and her emotional attachment to the Kaona's presented an ugly conflict she always thought wouldn't be an issue.

Unable to determine what happened to Jack's project proved to be a large setback for the FIS objective, especially after another few weeks of searching for the signal around town and in adjacent cities.

Bill agreed, with input from his recruiter Ron, to suspend the investigation until further notice. He gave the team instructions to keep an eye out and be ready, and then moved the team to inactive status.

Chapter 15

Glass Box

Enum prepared the next universe for Maya to learn from and this time promises it to be unlike prior experiences. To achieve this, without raising suspicion, Enum ensures the chaos theory solution is running before Maya steps into the wormhole.

The transport room darkens to a pitch black when the door closes. Moments later, as Maya begins to find comfort in optic deprivation, the blue runway lights flip on and gradually begin to glow at the highest intensity possible at this level. Ambient light from the wireframe transport floods the room, reflecting off every surface, and energizes Maya in the process.

Without further delay, the portal opens up and Maya slips through to a new realm.

This world is extremely different from others she has visited before. Normally the others were structured in ways similar to her home universe, with three-dimensional objects, five senses, and similar properties of physics.

She felt physically flat and oppressed for reasons she couldn't quite understand. The ground was bright white and extended for what appeared to be miles in all directions. A black bar taking up half of the horizon contrasted the ground and a dark, glossy sky which looked like a dome.

Maya froze in place, shocked and scared, confused at this world. She started to hear a very low ticking noise with a cadence timed to seconds.

"I don't understand," she says, and realizes, "Oh weird, it sounds like I'm talking under water. What is this strange place?"

Maya laughs maniacally after saying, "bub, bub, bubble."

Suddenly, a strange red bar appeared on the horizon, which was slightly longer than the black bar, and pushed its way through. The red bar progressively moved closer with every tick until passing right through her and disappearing.

"Alright, between the noise and those bars, it really seems like I'm in a flattened clock, at the bottom of an ocean," Maya claimed while pressing her lips firmly together and raising her cheeks with an unimpressed smile.

"Enum, where did you send me now, I'm in a realm where shadow meets light?" She blurted out expecting an answer, but the machine can only observe data and her question met with silence.

For some reason, Maya's question caused Enum to invoke a recall directive which sent part of the message to a typewriter in the room on the other side.

It's a mostly accurate observation though, Enum placed Maya into a two-dimensional world inside of a clock, but this was no ordinary clock. It isn't at the bottom of the sea and she can only hear two out of three dimensions of sound.

The second dimension is different to Maya than it would to a two-dimensional being. She is a three-dimensional being and can visualize in three dimensions without a problem. However, she loses some of her senses in two dimensions.

Anything in a second dimension is not able to visualize her third. Incidentally, this is much like a three dimensional being trying to look at a fourth dimensional being and will only see three of the four dimensions present; which is a most peculiar situation indeed.

Maya tried walking toward the black bars to see if anything else existed in this universe. As she walked, the clock face spun like a disc, where the edge, lined with numbers, moved behind her and the black bar on the horizon remained distant.

Once again, with the ticking noise, the red bar sweeps around and through Maya existence in the realm.

With frustration mounting, she belted out blistering screams at the top of her lungs. Yet the noise, muffled by the second dimension's inability to resonate a third dimension of sound, instead sounded like she was yelling under water.

Despite the minimally emphatic sound of frustration, the low-pitch noise seemed to work. Vibrations from her sound waves made the clock hands to stick together by forcing the center wheel pivot off axis because Maya's sounds were three-dimensional refracting in only two.

The clock froze at seven on the dot with its second hand stuck nearby ticking the same second over and over again.

Then, catching Maya by surprise, the sky lightened like a fast sunrise. She looked upward through the dome to see a large door opening followed by a pull-chain noise; the sky turned brighter with a warm white tinge to it. Her father, who appears to be fifty times larger, stands next to a desk near the light.

Maya could not believe her eyes.

She stared at Jack in shock and disbelief, trying to wrap her head around what her eyes are looking at. "Tell me how that's possible." She thought while expecting an answer from her conscious. Two ideas came to mind, one is her father came back to life and the other involves traveling back in time to witness an event.

Somehow the scenario selection by Enum placed Maya in a potentially paradoxical event. If she did manage to get her father's attention, the outcome of future happenings would easily be jeopardized if she warned him of, Julia's or his own, imminent death. At least, this is how she now perceived Jack's transformation in an orb of light, as a final existence.

Maya recalled another scenario, where she witnessed her mother's demise, and viewed it in similar light. She thought about the event as if she happened to know future at the time. Instead of witnessing the tragic event from a roof top, she may have decided to save her mother rather than see how she ends.

Enum is aware these challenging situations face the prospect of paradox, but the machine is calibrated to take those into account. If a paradox event occurs in a wormhole scenario, the program is designed to expunge guests from a virtual reality while simultaneously folding the scenario into nothingness. Furthermore, the way scenarios are constructed specifically to guide a subject along a predetermined path with an anticipated learning result.

She looked up toward the sky and freaked out saying, "Dad! Dad! Can you hear me?"

Her father was visible in the dome lens, very gigantic and optically warped, on the other side of the clock. He was in a storage shed, with a single light on, paging through file folders.

Maya reached up and pounded on the glass, creating a ripple in the space-time fabric into her father's universe. At that moment she learned the clock edges were no taller than her. Maya frantically tried to get Jack's attention, flailing about in a panicked state.

While she was fixated on getting her dad's attention, Maya failed to notice a hand of the clock reactivated to tick closer and closer to where she was standing. In a bizarre moment, the second-hand struck Maya, knocking her to the ground.

***

The next day, Maya awoke early at 7 am, in a fog from a twelve-hour slumber with phantom pain resonating after last night's event. She had trouble telling if the clock scenario was a scenario or a dream. For the immediate moment, it feels like a waking dream washing across her being as she is unable to tell what reality is anymore.

She is now more revitalized than any other time in her life, despite her confusion over reality, and her mind is in a state of clairvoyance able to extend confidence to entirely new levels. The rest supercharged Maya's awareness – she is ready to continue training, this is her new reality.

After exiting the amenities room, Maya approached the constants computer to setup the next transport. "Good morning to you, Enum." She says with a refreshing tone.

"Maya, welcome. I trust the rest has helped realign things for you." Enum responds.

"Yes! I haven't thought this clearly about anything for as long as I can remember. I certainly have to take advantage of the amenities again. It's probably a good time to start the next exercise." Maya confidently replied.

"Very well," Enum states and then opens the transport room.

A wormhole to a strange universe appears. This time, Enum prepared a special reality where a chaos theory solution meets a specific limitation, which is a concept of transcending intelligence from mechanical housings to biological matter.

As the instant colors of the new universe fade into realistic view, Maya understands she is in a very different situation. Portions of the setting are familiar, just like in previous realms, but the shape of this one is at odds.

She is standing in a white laboratory with multiple trapezoidal-shaped work stations. The room's walls do not form rectangles or squares. Instead, the room is irregular and asymmetric with the widest part being the floor she stands on.

Everything else about the lab seems to fit stereotypical characteristics often associated with a mad scientist's lair; including sophisticated arrangements of beakers, flasks, evaporator tubes and burners. The glass containers are irregularly shaped also, suggesting specific properties of this universe are not entirely visible.

In fact, Maya is in a universe which crosses planes with another. The shapes are distorted by warping of the space-time fabric and the human eye is incapable bending the light back into something a little more symmetric.

Subjects in the lab, placed on each of the experiment tables, are also asymmetric with their environment. Each subject is an area that artificial intelligence has difficulty beyond the mechanical sense.

Affecting animal, plant, or human biology requires a more complicated approach than other computer systems or machines. The underlying biological code is different from languages man created to allow machines to manipulate physical objects.

Yet, there are similarities between biology and machines, that one day in the future, mankind may acknowledge. Firstly, life is a product of the environment which creates according to the rules of nature even if it believes otherwise.

Secondly, science observes nature to create scientific solutions. Electrical circuits in a machine form neural network paths similar to that of the brain. Signals travel throughout the subsystems with information much like neurons in the human body.

Lastly, humans and machines both require energy supply to function; which is obtained from the immediate environment. Incidentally, it gives either the ability to control each other, by means of controlling the energy supply.

These commonalities make it possible for artificial intelligence to understand the physical compositions of life, but it lacks in an ability to understand thought and reaction. Heuristics teach machines possible outcomes; however, it may not be able to account for pure spontaneity.

"This has to be the oddest and strangest place I've ever seen." Maya says while biting her bottom lip with quiver of uncertainty if she should be there or not.

One station is setup in a peculiar fashion using chemical tubes running to a living palm tree placed under a high-intensity pyramid grow light. A computer is hooked up to the palm tree with a series of wire leads, almost as though a scientist was running thought experiments on it using a brain-net.

Equally strange to chemical tubes feeding a rainbow of fluids to the palm tree is a set of wire antennas protruding from the palm's trunk and fronds to enhance sensory capability.

It's common to measure environmental factors, such as temperature or moisture levels, as a way of determining what a plant needs or lacks. However, with live gene editing, this lab is setup to physically affect the plant's biological structure, manipulate how it perceives its environment, and allow it to make intelligent decisions.

The palm acknowledges Maya's presence by leaning to one side, rotating and tilting a frond vertically, then waves to her.

Shocked and fascinated, she responds to the palm after seeing a name tag in the container, "Why hello there, Foxtail."

The palm tree raises another frond, waves in the same way as before and shrugs, then lowers both fronds together. The nearby computer outputs text on the screen reading, "In reality, my name is Tulu, despite that scientific name printed on the tag, Wodyetia bifurcata, Foxtail."

Dumbfounded at the distraught plant, Maya replies, "Tulu, hello. Sorry, I didn't know."

Tulu types, "It's alright. I probably could have let you know in an introduction if my maker would just give me a voice. I hope I'm not the strangest thing you've seen, wait until you see the rats!"

"Rats?" Maya questions while thinking how much more bizarre that could be considering she's currently having a conversation with a palm tree.

Tulu raises a frond, turns, and points to the next lab desk.

A lab mouse testing station is next to the plant area and setup in a similar way. Several mice are in an enclosed transparent container, each with a tiny metal antenna sticking out of the skull. The antennas work like the plant versions on the adjacent lab desk, to receive and emit radio frequency waves to and from a laptop on the desk near the container.

Maya walks over to the mouse station and notices the mischief scurry into a corner. At first the mice looked afraid, but they were positioned in a specific formation, each a half-inch apart and staggered in a triangle shape. Their heads were tilted to once side to point the antennas at a receiver next to the container.

The computer hooked up to the receiver turned the monitor on and lines of text flooded the screen, scrolling page by page. Maya was able to read a few sentences as they clipped by and couldn't believe her eyes. The mice went on talking with each other after first acknowledging her.

"State your business human," Button says.

"Who are you?" Chip asks.

"Do you have food for us?" Ella questioned.

Ink responds to Ella, "No, does it look like she has any food?"

"How do you know it's a she? She could be a boy human." Noel says to Ink.

"Another day in a glass box," Rex says.

"Hi! My name is Maya, and I don't have any food, but I do feel hungry." she says to the mischief, followed by, "How are you doing?" with a puzzled look on her face as though she can't believe she's talking to a group of mice.

Then again, it's not too crazy considering a plant told her about the mice moments ago.

"Hey, we are not food." Button affirms.

"She's not eating us." Noel tells Button.

"We don't have food, and she doesn't have food, we're all out of luck," Says Ella.

"Maya could get us a tray of algae over there." Rex casually mentions.

"Don't tell her about the algae. I want something good." Ella responds to Rex.

"Oh, you must try the algae!" Ink says while turning his antenna to point at another lab desk.

Maya looked over at the desk Ink pointed to. A trapezoid-shaped incubator warms several hexagon petri dishes, which are stacked on top of each other, on a specialized racking system. Wires run from each dish to a centralized bundle which then hooks up to a computer next to the incubator; she walks over for a closer look.

The petri dish computer was different from the mouse and plant computers. No conversations were on the screen to provide her feedback about what's going on in the dishes. Instead, the monitor displayed a number of environment metrics in graphs at the top, and a very curious section of information right below it.

An algorithm applied to the algae allows control over other organisms in the array. For example, algae can tap into dishes with bacteria present for accelerated growth and flocculation.

The algae may also access viral culture dishes to test immunities and build defenses.

In other words, these algae are able to replicate, improve survival, and group together at paces determined by an artificial intelligence. Feedback on the screen demonstrates an adaptive learning capability where the algorithm has successfully modified the efficiency of a living microorganism.

A revolution is slowly brewing inside the irregular incubator by way of computer-assisted algorithms. The algae have developed efficient ways to leverage bacteria in a mutually beneficial relationship while defending against virus dishes. Evidently, the algae evolved with certain features in the closed environment which allows them to mimic viral properties.

Maya looked at the terminal and noticed similar settings to the financial market's computer from an earlier adventure. These settings allow her to override information passed to the algae for learning and lab evolution. She contemplated running the anti-algorithm, wondering how bad it could be with a self-contained system.

The temptation hovered in her mind like a desire for candy after tasting it for the first time. Hell broke loose in the previous scenario, but she still believed it was because she wasn't prepared for it despite what Enum told her. Now that she is ready for an unforeseen outcome, would things work out better this time?

A series of automated controls took over right before Maya had a chance to give the anti-algorithm another attempt. "No, no, don't!" She yelled at the incubator.

The algae evolved to enhanced capability before her eyes, with an ability to send electrical impulses back to the computer; they managed to find a way past directive communications by help of the learning algorithm.

She could tell something wasn't right at the moment they took over and feared for the worst. Much like the stock market flat-line, vital signs and environment feedback metrics all dropped to zeros. The anti-algorithm switched on, seemingly by itself, and the mice cowered into a corner.

Maya witnessed, first-hand, an amazing technological achievement where microorganisms learned how to transcend a mechanical barrier. The algae have literally given the computer a virus, except this virus is made of energy and not in the form of malicious code.

"Curses to hades," Maya says in angst while clinching her eyes shut and shaking closed fists in the air.

By this time, anything she could do to stave off the escalating tragedy is too reactionary to be effective. Instead of triage, she figured it was best to wait it out until Enum closes the wormhole and sends her back to the home universe.

Every minute passing increased her anxiety level and Maya grew impatient with waiting for a transport home. She feared more than the worst now, while observing a biological virus take over the entire lab's computer systems.

An unexpected transformation inside the incubator presented a brand-new concern. Algae began multiplying at an alarming rate, to the point the growing formation covered the container walls and proceeded to make its way into the lab.

On top of hyper-multiplication, the algae appeared to be consuming material as it moved forward, followed by a thick line of glowing ember and ash; the smell is putrid and sweet like burning sugar.

Chatter on the mice monitor started to look like troll spam from chat bots, and it cycled across the screen as quickly as thoughts raced through Maya's head. The mice were freaking out at the destruction unfolding and no human could read all of those lines fast enough to understand.

The intelligent palm tree thought it was in its best defense to shed the antennas and grow bark on the leaves to act as armor, thus preventing the virus from leaping to it too. Instead of talking, it remained silent to conserve energy.

While the palm played armadillo, the mice put their antennas together. An electrostatic shield bubble immediately formed around the mischief when all antennas touched. The mice too, were taking a ball-like defense approach to danger.

Maya was equally afraid of the impending doom, but she did not have a way to seal off from the lab environment. She quickly looked around for anything that could protect her from the virus. "A conveniently placed hermetic lab outfit would be right as rain right now," she said in a sarcastic tone.

She looked in cabinets and closets, only finding lab coats and miscellaneous unhelpful lab supplies. Maya thought how odd it is, considering the type of experiments, not a single piece of safety equipment anywhere.

"I suppose this is it. I might as well put a bag over my head," she claimed in defeat.

Then, while glancing across the room, she spotted a tall white garbage bin tucked under the palm tree lab desk. "Well, it's better than nothing."

Maya ran over to the desk, turned the bin over, and pulled the garbage bag out. She emptied the bag's contents on the floor, then folded and pressed the bag flat before placing it by her feet.

She then stood on the bag, put the refuse bin over her head and squatted. Unfortunately, it isn't quite large enough to fit her whole body; her feet and ankles are still exposed.

The mice monitor scrolled with laughter as they thought refuse bin is incredibly inferior to an electrostatic shield – plus they could see her feet and believed her actions were amusing to watch.

The palm tree remained silent throughout.

Soon the smell of consumed material was exhaustingly strong. Maya knew she didn't have much time before she too, would be consumed. Gas byproduct filling the air started entering her lungs – Maya then blacked out and fell over.

Chapter 16

The Key

Maya woke up on an examination table in the lab recovery chamber and noticed Enum was running a series of diagnostics on her condition. The previous scenario proved to be a little much for what her body could handle. She passed out from inhalation of toxic fumes escaping from the creeping bacteria, while taking cover in a garbage can, and didn't receive enough oxygen at the time.

The scenario possibly took things too far, but Enum knew Maya needed to experience the worst of what can happen when the anti-algorithm is set free to evolve with a mind of its own. This is where Maya progressed, from timid and mild situations, to facing the destructive force head-on.

When her electrolytes were back to a normal range, Maya began to feel like herself again and she attempted to communicate with Enum. She was ' experiencing confusion and generally felt discombobulated in the first few moments.

"Where am I? Why is the lab still here? Everything was being eaten alive by bacteria." Maya questioned in a frantic and concerning voice. "Why am I disheveled?"

Strangely, as attributed to the real parallel world she was just in, Maya's clothing had char marks along the edges. Her shoes, shirt sleeves and ankles, were all singed by the close call. A subtle, yet detectable smell filled the air similar to burning corn husks and wet dirt.

"You are safe, Maya. The most recent iteration of a parallel universe brought you to the brink of death to help you understand how powerful this knowledge can be. For a few moments, you were unconscious from the result." Enum replied.

Enum performed a series of calculations, in the span of a human breath, and then produced output on a nearby diagnostic monitor.

The machine continued after populating the screen, "Your vitals stabilized rather quickly after the incident. Electrolytes were administered as well as a comprehensive scan to identify any further issues."

Maya continued to have trouble recalling exactly what happened," Enum, how did I become unconscious? I am having trouble remembering."

"In the final moments of the scenario," said Enum while flipping the vitals monitor to information on the bacteria. "An organism found a way, with access to the anti-algorithm, to control a virus and grow at an exponential rate. When it reached a threshold capacity, the organism evolved its digestive system further, it found a way to breakdown mass and use the energy as fuel."

The monitor switched to a view of the bacteria creeping along the floor and Enum continued the review.

"This organism learned to ingest anything in its path like a very strong acid, reducing matter to ash, noxious gases, and water vapor. There wasn't much you could do, Maya. Covering yourself with a garbage receptacle only hastened things by causing the escaping gas to accumulate inside. When my vital alarm for low oxygen went off, I pulled you out of the scenario."

A tidal wave of shock and disbelief rushed over Maya's face. She was no longer concerned about being disheveled or why she woke up where she did. Instead she felt helpless to the power of a solution to chaos theory with a mind of its own.

"Enum, how would anyone prevent this, or any other scenario, from taking place? Everything seemed beyond my control, in every scenario, and I was too late to take corrective action." Maya questioned as she straightened her hair back into place with her fingers and adjusted her shirt.

The computer responded, "Exactly."

Maya replied in a frustrated tone, "Exactly what? What could I do?"

"For each of the scenarios, your goal is to understand exactly what you do now. The point here is that a solution to chaos theory must be protected at all costs. Any interaction with the outside world will cause destruction and leave shadows of chaos in its wake," Stated the machine.

Enum paused for a moment to let Maya absorb, and then said, "Essentially, all that needed to happen is to isolate the anti-algorithm and remove it from play."

"Oh wow, I really over-complicated what I thought I was supposed to do." Maya replied with wide eyes and a look of surprise.

Enum proceeded to wrap up the training with a final statement, "Yes, eliminate the source, by any means necessary. Simply prevent the medium from interacting with any device. Pull the USB dongle out, or unplug the Ethernet wire, or smash the WI-FI router if you have to. Only use it in a controlled environment where the outside world remains unaffected. If you remember this, and apply it, then your training has completed."

"Please rest for now and visit the control room when you are refreshed. I will now switch to privacy mode." Enum said.

Thinking about the prior scenarios, Maya now understood why Enum pushed her mental fitness while under duress. The unfavorable outcomes have etched into her memory and remain as vivid as though she was still right there. Given the recent information, one of the exercises bothers her more than the others. Where was the anti-algorithm device in the scenario about witnessing her mother's freak accident?

She replayed the experience over and over in her mind for an hour while relaxing in the recovery chamber. Maya looked for clues and reviewed her memory from as many different angles as possible.

Each time, she drew a blank and could not figure out how the anti-algorithm affected the outcome. She decided to thinking about other things for a while, to let her mind recoup, and have a nap to recharge.

A few hours later, Maya woke up to a very odd and realistic dream. She was standing on the top of a very tall building with several other skyscrapers around. The buildings wobbled and swayed from a force stronger than wind. They bent in flux, creating an arc shape far enough only the ground was visible below, as she grabbed a railing in fear of her life.

The swaying went on for several gyrations and then suddenly the buildings shattered. Maya could hear pieces of metal snapping, bricks cracking, and screams in the distance. Just before she snapped out of it, Maya was falling to the ground back-first with debris in the air around her.

It reminded her of a similar dream she had years ago. The situation was similar, with tall buildings in a downtown setting, except she was on the ground running away from tornadoes. People ran through the streets with her as destructive wind funnels went up and down the roads like trains on tracks. Maya felt there was no escape from the demise about to ensue.

Perhaps the dreams were predictions of the future and her relationship to the anti-algorithm. She thought maybe her mind has been trying to tell her, in all of these years, a warning of a life-threatening event to take place. Another possibility is Maya felt helpless and out of control of her life, and if she didn't regain control then chaos is on its way.

Despite trying to take her mind off the alternate universe experience with a gargoyle and her mother's vehicle, she still couldn't figure out where the anti-algorithm device was located, or how she could have prevented the accident.

After a quick bathroom break, Maya went over to the control room as Enum had instructed earlier. She quickly asked Enum the burning question before it started the dialog protocol. "Enum, in the other universe where I witnessed my mom's tragedy, exactly where was the anti-algorithm device? I tried to figure it out several times, but I'm not having much luck."

"Maya, it seems you might need additional training!" Enum replied with a smile emote on the screen.

She had an uneasy look on her face now and said, "By training, you mean I have to run the scenario again?"

"No. I recently installed a humor module and this was the first chance I had to apply it to a human." Enum responded.

Maya started laughing, not at the training joke, but because everything about Enum's statement just seemed ridiculous.

Enum continued, "The alternate universe you're talking about was a control experiment. In the control, I learn about your reactions to various stimuli and how you respond to emotionally-charged events. Then the data is analyzed and used to help build follow-up universe scenarios. No anti-algorithm device existed in that world and it is perceptive of you to ask."

A weight lifted off Maya's shoulders after realizing she worried about an unknown device for no apparent reason. The encounter is bothersome though and she felt like it was a clue to figuring out what really happened. Enum has other plans however and this isn't the time to investigate.

"There are further instructions and a path you must now take. I will display video from your father, his final wishes, and the completed anti-algorithm key will be available to you. Once taken, you must exit the facility. A sensor will lock down my system within ten minutes of the action and you will not be able to leave if you're inside when this happens," Enum stated.

"Maya, these are certainly exciting times. You have progressed through Enum's training sessions and are ready to embark on the world's greatest journey. I understand how much you have gone through to make it to this point and how difficult the adjustment can be. Years ago, when I was hardly around on the farm, I went through a very similar process in setting everything up for you," Jack told Maya in the farewell video.

Jack appeared to have a neurological disorder with subtle involuntary muscle twitches and sudden movements. His left eye was drooping, his lips quivered uncontrollably, and he blinked in sync with the twitching while talking.

Maya didn't notice the impairments when she'd last seen him alive and found it odd that his condition was worse in the past. The video was created in a much weaker moment of emotional intelligence, not long after the initial knowledge upload.

A large part of Maya's mental state is conflicted. The last time she spoke with her father was just before he took a backward dive off a cliff and turned into a glowing blue orb. It was incredibly strange then and is still strange now. Maya was reminded of the event by hearing her father's voice for the first time in a while. She thought she merely imagined he turned into an orb then and that none of the incident really happened.

Her father continued, "When I discovered a solution to chaos theory, I was not prepared for what it meant to the modern world. I was also not ready for the dangers associated with bringing a forbidden knowledge into the scientific limelight and thus why I had to part ways with society. My hope for you, through Enum's training, is to understand the mistakes I witnessed firsthand and learn how to adapt to those situations."

She questioned in her mind why he needed to leave that badly, and strand her with nobody to care, especially knowing she already lost her mother years ago. Maya thought maybe her desire to have loved ones around might be a bit selfish, considering the greater good, but the thought could not stop her from feeling the way she does.

Jack adds to his previous notion with another, "Of course, per Enum's protocol, the best solution is often a matter of neutralizing the impact of the anti-algorithm, but there are ways you can reshape society for positive benefit. You can correct wrongs before they happen without disrupting mankind's natural evolution in parallel with technology."

Maya felt uneasy about the suggestion of large-scale interference with society's evolving path. She has always seen life as a participant, rather than an architect, and prefers to stay clear of conflict. The impact of Enum's intelligence, and the anti-algorithm, is beginning to test her in ways she would intentionally avoid. In many ways she wanted to live a normal life, but she realized at an early age that it would be impossible.

"Why did you have to leave too?" She said to the likeliness of Jack while attempting to hold back tears.

It was impossible for Jack to respond to the question and coincidentally he was about to give a digest on why he had to leave.

Jack is now the one trying hard to fight back his emotions, "I know this is probably stirring up a lot of emotions over the family. Please understand Maya, this is larger than a few feelings our family shared while raising you into the strong and competent individual you turned out to be. Know that if there were any other way, which kept all of us together, I would have pursued it in a heartbeat. I love your mom and you very much."

Tears rolled down Maya's cheeks as she stared at the monitor. She stood motionless and lost in her father's words, and had finally allowed herself to cry. The feeling oozed through her body like volcano lava, hot with a smoldering aftermath, and liberated her from tension buried deep down below the surface.

"I know you know, since you made it this far, I have already left in a ball of blue light, a concentrated form of the energy I was made of, and my destiny made it so. The choice I made, to upload all of the world's information into my brain, put me on a collision course with the universal mind. I could not survive for long in this state before the universe would reclaim what is rightfully meant to be hidden from humans," He explained.

Maya was in shock, "You uploaded the world's information into your brain?"

Unable to hear her anyway, Jack kept his tape rolling, "I knew when and how. It didn't matter where I was at the time, but the universe set a time of reclamation. For you to understand the importance of what I had to ask of you, I chose for the final moment to be spent with you. If you were able to see something the world has never seen, then I could convince you solely by witnessing the universe taking its knowledge back."

Things were starting to make sense to Maya now. She understood her father took a risk with becoming the world's most knowledgeable person, but who knew it would ultimately destroy his life. It was precisely like Jack to have to know everything and to succumb to an overwhelming urge to understand why everything works the way it does.

Maya forgave her father for everything he did at that very moment. Pioneers of their time take incredible leaps to create a world outside of the box and her father is no different in this respect. Despite being sad and upset she lost him, Maya was impressed with her father and the lengths he went to in an effort to revolutionize the world; at least this much she could understand.

The video then showed Jack getting up from his seat at desk in Enum's control room. He walked over to a panel under the large panel monitor, found a small fingerprint sensor and pressed it gently. The panel opened and a tray holding a small polished metal wand slid outward.

After picking up the device, he said, "This object is the product of my life's work and my most protected secret. Inside the container is a completed anti-algorithm program ported to hundreds of system languages for deployment. The universe may eventually reclaim its knowledge, but this program is capable of changing human existence forever and finally put us in a superior position over the architecture of life."

He wrapped his hand around the box, placing four fingers and a thumb in matching grooves which each have a sensor in them. With the right pressure, and another fingerprint scan, the small box opened a tiny hole at one end. The device switched on and a beam of jumbled computer code in blue light projected onto the wall nearby.

"What looks like valid code in projection is actually an incomplete logic. This is a final deterrent designed to keep the secret if someone else made it here before you. They, as in a hypothetical group threatening my project, who may have been able to hypothetically cut my hand off and unlock the panel."

The video went black for a second and then started back up again.

"Also, the code cannot be completed by Enum alone using video analysis. There is a trick for reading the code and it requires a part of who you are," Jack said while trying to contain his excitement over the enhanced security features.

Jack then tells the artificial intelligence, "Enum, start deciphering protocol."

The lights turn off. Only the jumbled computer code illuminates the control room. Jack turns the device toward the projection screen and says, "Enum, please decipher and enumerate code languages on the device."

Enum responds, "Deciphering now, please wait."

Around twenty seconds lapse before Enum says, "Deciphering complete. Updating device and securing for Maya."

"Update is complete. Device secured and registered to Maya Kaona's biometric profile," Enum added only a few seconds later.

"Do you want me to continue by listing the code languages?" The machine questioned.

Jack replied, "Only to disk, no audio, thank you."

Over the course of the demonstration, he gradually sounded more and more rushed and impatient. It was difficult for Maya to understand why there's a sudden level of desperation in Jack's voice or why it seemed like he was wrapping up the video this way. She thought maybe the stress is getting to him or that an outside influence might be affecting him.

"Maya, you will need Enum to unlock the device before continuing. As part of the enhanced security protocol, you will have a very short time to leave the premises with the device before full lock-down commences. Please do not remember this as our final farewell; we will see each other again in the future. It is your time to save the world and bring about positive change on a global scale," stated Jack.

"I must go now. Oh, and Maya, there is one more thing. People of the world believe they are in control of everything, but little do they know it is the objects they create in control of them."

The video ended right then, paused on a frame of Jack's last words to Maya before they'd speak again later on a hill near the family farm. She stared at the image, both at Jack and the background, thinking she might be able to find a clue about his sporadic behavior. Everything appeared as it is now except Jack wasn't sitting at his desk.

Enum returned to an active state and popped open the airlock panel as code directive embedded at the end of the video. Maya walked over and picked up the device from the panel tray. She wrapped her hand around the device, squeezed her fingers into the biometric sensors, and projected a green light onto the wall.

Though she was unsure of how to attain her goal, Maya made up her mind about what needed to be done next. She was bitter over what this knowledge did to her family, but hopeful of how the device could change the world for the better. It was time for her to stop wavering and take action; she needed it to end now.

"Please unlock the device for me, Enum," She said with a confidence unlike any Enum has heard before.

"Very well, Maya," Enum replied while unlocking the device.

The computer continued, "There is a vehicle fueled up and ready for you in the building's garage. Proceed to parking lot floor level-D, by the elevator, and take the vehicle parked in space seventy. A fingerprint unlocks the door and. further instruction will follow."

She ran over to her living quarters, grabbed a spare set of clothes and her survival backpack, and then exited the facility to the elevator. On the way down, Maya thought about how awesome it would be to see the sun for the first time in what felt like forever. She had been cooped up in the lab so long she lost track of time. Traveling to other universes also messed with her body clock and the next few days would be an adjustment.

Chapter 17

Vortex

Jack hardly anticipated the implication for suddenly having access to an enormous amount of data. Though tired from long days wrestling with sanity, he began to notice specific phenomena he couldn't see before. This is the blessing in disguise, a seemingly unintended consequence of learning everything, an ability to pool information and find another reality within reality itself.

An underlying thread, running through all of mankind's computerized data, is a theme of perception. There are people who believe life mostly unfolds beyond control and randomness is a large factor. There are others who believe they're in complete control and the idea of randomness is mere fabrication used to explain the unexplained.

Examining how people perceive random events opened an incredibly large door for Jack, because he could plainly see nothing is random in the data. Everything had many factors which lead to an eventual outcome, and most people were not able to see all of these factors, only the outcome resonated. A series of events took place each time to produce what could be perceived as random.

An example is the global financial market where stocks fluctuate primarily on news and investor relations. The stocks are still affected by millions of different data points that charts hardly encompass.

Suppose several thousand investors own a majority of stock, enough to sway the share price and each one of those investors has a number of factors going on in their everyday lives. One might sell out of financial need while another buys using extra money from a merit increase.

On the outside it may look as random, since it's difficult to know exact reasons at the individual investor level, but the number of factors comes into play whether or not other investors or firms know it. Charts look at majority movements, for key signals, using mathematics to help find a predictable pattern or at least a general direction on which way the curve is heading.

Knowing all factors changes everything.

Jack can look historically at any symbol and see all factors leading to a movement in share price. He isn't quite in a real-time position yet, but the archival data is plenty enough to understand what exactly is going on when the whole picture is considered. Essentially, every factor is a new pixel in an incredibly high-resolution image.

The same applies to lottery games, which are gambled on odds to a truer sense of randomness that a specific series of numbers will turn up on draw night out of millions of possible combinations.

Funny enough to Jack, when looking at all of the factors, he is able to see why the numbers turned up as they did. He examined everything from the individual ball density, to the timing of ball release, right down to what the number caller had for lunch that day.

He took everything he learned from case studies and applied it to create the most sinister of all evils, an anti-algorithm. Ironically, the anti-algorithm is an algorithm of sorts, which is capable of removing randomness from formulas by replacing those elements with heuristic factors. Instead of guessing at possible outcomes trying to match random seeds, Jack can apply artificial intelligence to look at results ahead of time, as quickly as sensor data pours in.

Critically, the supercomputer must be able to aggregate a huge dataset, from billions of data points, and then process everything with the groundbreaking formula quickly enough to provide a person with actionable intelligence. Gathering data on how the formula processes information is then analyzed to understand how a large number of factors determined a potential outcome.

From the research, Jack discovered a way to essentially predict any future actions dependent on human intervention at some point. With that information, he was able to transform the formula into a solution for one of the most evasive questions of mankind, a solution for chaos theory.

A solution to chaos theory isn't something to be put lightly by any means, because the implication of this knowledge changes everything humans understand about existence. For example, one could sit on a sunny beach and watch waves roll up along the shoreline to relax. While watching the waves, with chaos theory applied to hydrodynamics, the person can tell exactly where the next wave would break and exactly how far up the beach it would travel.

Another person could look at trees in autumn and describe when each leaf would fall to the ground, and where each leaf would land, while considering all factors such as changing temperatures and wind turbulence.

The trick however, for supporting the fundamental heuristic side of the anti-algorithm, is an ability to read as many data points from the environment as possible. Perhaps the scary part of that is how all of those sensor inputs are already readily available to human senses without a need for bionic enhancement; the human brain is capable of super-sensory aggregation when unlocked to its fullest potential.

Exactly how Jack found the idea, which lead to an evolutionary leap in human intelligence, may be attributed to an interaction long ago with Bill Westgate. Years before Westgate's Garage was in dire straits, Jack would visit Bill on a regular basis for oil changes and car maintenance. The visits provided time for Jack and Bill to chat and get up to speed with things going on in each other's lives.

One conversation in particular could be considered the seed to Jack's quest of solving chaotic theory.

Jack asked, "Don't you get antsy out here, Bill?"

Bill was lying on a creeper under Jack's car, cranking the oil filter bolt back into place, listening. After tightening the bolt, he wiped off the filter with a red shop rag and rolled out from underneath the vehicle.

"I think it might drive me bonkers after a while, being out here all alone," Jack added.

Bill stood up, nodding to acknowledge the question, and proceeded using the dirty rag to clean oil off the socket wrench.

"I watch life go by so slowly out here, Jack. Even with a little work dribbling in, I actually enjoy having it this way better. I've gotten used to having more time on my hands out here in the boonies compared to running the garage in Elm Woods." Bill stated with a content smile and a raspy voice.

He paused for a second to blow a spurt of air into the socket and continued, "It makes me happy, to see life unfold at a pace I'm capable of keeping up with, you know? I have Shadow to keep me company, and strangely, I think she feels the same way."

Jack perked up from a draining disposition and said, "I can only imagine what I would do with enough time to be able to hear myself think. I'm seriously considering a more reclusive lifestyle, even-though being busy can be motivating."

Bill looked at Jack in a perplexed way, "Oh I couldn't go back to the busy way things were. Existing is the only motivation I need, really. In all of this time too, I've managed to get a handle on myself and understand what my life is."

Then, without speaking, Bill walked over to the bay door, opened it by pressing an up-button, and bright light poured into the garage area. Jack took the action as a cue he might be chatting too much right now for Bill's current state of mind to desire hearing.

"Sounds really intriguing, are you going to elaborate? You have me curious now." Jack questioned while seeking details.

"I sure can," replied Bill. "I'm actually quite proud of my hypothesis, you know, for being a dumb mechanic who lives in the middle of nowhere." He says with a laugh.

Jack found it amusing too and shared in the laugh. He knows Bill is smart, well-educated, and conveys a demeanor which often fools people who judge him by looks. In fact, intelligence is a common ground between the two friends and they tend to stay on the same wavelength because of it.

"Life is a food. It can be complicated or simple, tasty or disgusting, hot or cold." Bill said while widening his eyes.

He refined the thought further by saying, "As with food, there are a number of ingredients mixed together in different ways, to create varying sensations on our tongues and in our stomachs. With life, there are a number of particles mixed together in different ways, to create sensations and thoughts in our minds and memories."

Jack realized in that moment, the deep and profound direction Bill was heading, and blurted out, "Brings a whole new meaning to food for thought," in attempt to lessen the depth a little.

Bill laughed, "Why yes it does! It was right there, I can't believe I didn't think of that one before you did. I know it's deep, maybe too deep for the needs of scientific method, but life is the result of a recipe if you really think about it."

"I would have to agree. The world, and matter itself, is made with billions of tiny elements. Everything is a specific combination of elements arranged in certain ways to create life and objects." Jack replied with an increasing level of excitement and speed in his voice as he continued talking.

"Bill, this is incredible, the tangent of thought you've put me on. I could go on for hours thinking about it now; DNA soup!"

"Oh, I don't want to downplay it too much when you're this excited, but I really think it's just another way of looking at the entirety of life." Bill responded while trying to deflate the conversation.

Jack quickly replies, "Nope, no worries there. You are correct and I probably should let it fester for a while before concluding a new outlook, eh? We wouldn't want to get ahead of ourselves."

As time passed after the encounter, Jack steadily kept the notion of life's recipes in the back of his mind, entertaining the idea every once in a while. Eventually it would lead to a broader understanding of the universe and all things contained within it; almost to a point it seems oversimplified.

Casual conversations between Jack and Bill rarely exposed personal agendas to either party. Both men treaded with caution, knowing their intelligence is at times enough cause for alarm, but they truly enjoyed batting around hypothetical concepts. Knowledge remains a competitive barrier, despite how long they've been friends, and any chance to run with an idea took precedence over loyalty.

There is a certain level of distrust which the men cannot shake when they think about their friendship. The paranoia, though intentionally suppressed on both sides during confrontations to present a level of civility, stems from the fountain of knowledge. Both men believe knowledge is power and that being selective about what is shared is the smartest way to protect personal intentions.

Jack invested a lot of time and energy into building his secret empire of computerized intelligence. He felt free to share benefits of sophisticated automation with companies and end users, but was very stingy in discussing the inter-workings of his technologies.

He protected core functionality like trade secrets simply to prevent anyone from catching up to his level; he considered Bill as someone who might impede progress.

The technologies served a greater purpose, as a means to an end, which Jack could barely fathom before realization. Every accomplishment brought him a step closer to understanding questions mankind spent centuries trying to answer. There's no logical way that he could describe, to allow anyone else to attain this level of knowledge before he did.

Fortunately, for the fate of the world, Jack employed the same mantra when arriving at a solution to chaos theory. Not a single soul could know what he learned and it became his sole responsibility to protect the knowledge from outside discovery.

"In my being, this power is a burden I am not ready to shoulder. Yet I also cannot destroy the knowledge for it may be responsibly used by future humans who have learned to harness its potency." Jack claimed as he devised steps to ensure the anti-algorithm is secured from all to find.

He decided it was best to pass down the knowledge to his daughter, Maya. The way this knowledge is transferred would teach her about the dangers of it falling into the wrong hands and that ultimately, she must pass it along too. Jack felt sick, knowing the stress it would place on his daughter next, but there is no other person he could trust more.

To make matters complex, yet workable for Maya to decipher, the anti-algorithm was split into pieces which could only be found by her thought process alone. As he developed the puzzle, Jack spent time teaching Maya fun things about science on the family farm while seeding answers she would need later. Maya helped in building practical automation devices, her father engineered, to make life easier on the farm.

The crucial part of how the anti-algorithm would be passed relied on Maya's curiosity and understanding of life. She adapted quickly to a scientific-minded family as she grew up and always asked questions about things she was attempting to understand. For example, Maya had a profound interest in physics by the time she was ten years old and would often look for ways to apply it to problems.

Automation on the farm kicked into high gear after Julia's unfortunate accident; because Jack knew the farm would be a lot more sweat for one person to handle and had a need to make life better for Maya. Previously, mom and daughter were able to get mostly everything completed with a little hard work and a few fully automated tasks. Jack would help out every now and then too; he wasn't completely missing in action.

Maya ended up in a difficult position though. Instead of spending time with friends she went home after school each night to pitch in and keep the farm running. Eventually this meant forgoing post-secondary school in college and working full-time on the farm. She really didn't mind skipping college to stay home and tend to family business; it gave her freedom without the stress of being evaluated for showing up.

For safety, Jack also let Maya know about the civil tension and competition for knowledge between Bill and himself. Jack made it clear for Maya to understand, that despite Bill's candor and charm, ulterior motives exist below the surface. It was the first warning to Maya which detailed how the information she learns from her father is meant to be closely guarded secrets.

The majority of what Jack knows about Bill is only on the surface and it's exactly how he intends to keep the secrecy of a double-life. While he appears to be mostly uninvolved with the world outside of the garage, Bill is a man who operates on ulterior motives and is always thinking ahead to snuff out a fire before it sparks.

Former military training placed Bill in contact with officials at high levels of government and put him in a hush position to fulfill special operations contracts, despite not moving up the chain of command as far as he anticipated. This secret agency, funded through defense spending, seeks to leverage intelligent mindsets for tasks involving cutting-edge scientific research.

Contracts only include black-book targets, meaning no agents beyond the unit knew about the activities or who carried them out, and the agency functions without a name or archived documentation. He viewed the agency as a for-those-who-know operation as part of a shadow government. Though he enjoyed running secret operations, Bill felt trapped by contributing. Any deviation or attempt to expose the secrets would instantly put his life in jeopardy.

Jack could read between the lines and knew there was more to Bill than fixing cars in the middle of nowhere. He would prod for clues during conversations, often enough and subtle, but was quick to dial it down when Bill seemed to be picking up on the technique. Jack knew Bill had to have at least an inkling of his attempts to find out what Bill is really up to.

Throughout the years, gathering research and intelligence for the agency, Bill worked with a man by name of Ron Barker on a few missions. Ron was stationed with Bill during three combat deployments, seven undercover reconnaissance missions, before moving on to become a senior level operative in the agency. He periodically assigned tasks to Bill, like other senior members, and collaborated on highly classified operations.

When he first heard about Jack's work, Ron quickly moved to bring Bill on board. He showed up at the Silverville garage for a private talk and it didn't take a whole lot of convincing to push Bill into the mix.

Ron walked to the screen door on the porch and knocked on the wood frame. Shadow barely acknowledged Ron's presence, which was typical.

"Jax, it has certainly been a while. What brings you all the way out here?" Bill questioned with enthusiasm, using Ron's military nickname to address him.

The nickname stuck with Ron since basic training, shortly after he first joined a squad as the biggest, chiseled muscle man any of the guys had seen before. When he walked into formation, a private whispered to a buddy about how jacked Ron looked and the commander was unimpressed by the incident.

"What are you saying there, private? You might as well tell the squad now since you've interrupted the training. Get down, give me fifty, and tell everyone what is so important you had to talk while in formation." The commander said in a piercingly sharp tone without really raising his voice at all.

The private started doing push-ups and spoke while facing the dirt, "I said, that guy is jacked!"

"I can't hear you! I mean, literally, I can't hear you. Get your face out of the dirt boy, your squad is not in the dirt yet, turn your head and tell them what you said," replied the commander as he grew agitated.

After turning his head sideways, the private tried to yell this time, while straining from his push-ups, "I said! That guy is Jaxxed!"

The commander snapped back, "Darn right he is, it's apparent he likes to get jaxxed, just look at how Jax he is!"

A good test of a man's character is not by what he is able to accomplish, but instead by how he strategically refrains from conflict. This is his attitude, a disciplined man, who knows when it's appropriate to get in involved. Ron stood there as if he wasn't just made the center of attention by another soldier, staring right ahead, without even a flinch at the comment.

"It's been a long-ass time, man. The only one who still calls me Jax is you," replied Ron.

Bill looks unconvinced and says, "Hey, you're still pretty pumped up there, I would say it applies."

"Can I come in? I know we're out in the boonies, but it's a good idea to continue following protocol for what I have to say, do you have a secure area?" Ron asked.

Ron went inside and followed Bill down a set of stairs to a dank basement operations room across the hallway from an underground chop shop.

The room is filled with various equipment and materials used for surveillance, which also happens to be wired throughout the garage for monitoring. If anyone were snooping around the shop, the cameras and devices would pick it up fast enough to give time for escape if need be.

He grabbed a seat next to a work table, looked around, and told Bill, "Nice setup! Good to know you keep to your communications training side. Let me get straight to the point here."

Bill decided he might as well sit too. It's not every day a former military buddy stops by like this so he figured it was probably serious.

"This is about as secure as it's going to get here. I don't have access to the right equipment to make it pro, though we're inside a Faraday Cage, so at least there are no air signals in or out." Bill stated.

Ron looked around the room again at the stainless-steel wire mesh covering the walls, floor, and ceiling. "It might be a little overkill for way out here, but it's wise not to take the risk."

After repositioning in the chair to face Bill at a better angle, Ron continued, "Alright, well, here goes. I moved up to an integral part in the First Intelligence Syndicate. I know it's been some time since your last operation with FIS, but I really think you can help us out on this one."

Bill nods and says without hesitation, "Yes, count me in. Things have been a little dry around here and some action will do me well."

"I figured as much, but you know, it's polite to qualify, at least I believe so." Ron replied.

He then stuck his hand in a pocket, fished around for a few seconds, and pulled out a wallet-size photo of Jack Kaona.

Ron showed Bill the photo and questioned, "I understand you know who this man is, Jackson Thomas Kaona?"

He paused for a moment.

"FIS learned about Mr. Kaona after a series of radio frequency interruptions. These were very brief transmissions, but enough to be cause for concern with the syndicate as the action disrupted key communication channels."

The syndicate did not know or understand the full scope of what they discovered. Each signal discovered was an evolving end-point of the Enum supercomputer; which was designed to transcend energy networks. Radio interference is sometimes a byproduct as the artificial intelligence increases its physical footprint.

Curious how Jack could have done this, Bill asked, "I've met him a few times, and he's helped me out with the land lease, but I'm not sure if he's capable of signal jamming. Are you sure?"

"Oh yes, highly suspect, FIS associated him to the incidents. With triangulation, the search narrowed to a series of emitters, which appeared to be remote relays for a much larger system. Mr. Kaona's owns several properties involved and we know from his farm automation that he possesses the scientific mentality required."

"Investigation into the source revealed a phenomenon like never seen before."

Ron cleared his throat. He seemed to be losing train of thought and Bill could hear tension escalating in his raspy voice.

He spoke more candidly, "Of all the strange things I've seen in my career, this by far tops the list. I wish it wasn't as severe as it is, really, I do, but this has the ability to wipe out entire armies and governments. My nerves are on edge thinking the problem is out there now, and it's growing as we speak."

"Well, I know what might help with that," Bill replies while reaching under the desk to grab a bottle of whiskey.

"This ought to calm the nerves a bit; I keep a ten-year close for times like these."

He thumps the bottle on the desk and then pulls two glasses from a small wicker basket next to where the bottle rested in a thick layer of dust.

Ron breaks a firm look on his face with a slight smile, "I'm not going to argue with that."

Bill blew the dust out of each glass and off the bottle. Fine particles filled the air and swirled around in the light from a basement window. They slowly fell back to the desk like floating feathers.

"It's not a tendency for me to drink, I get a headache damn near every time, but I use it once in a while as a tool to change my frame of mind," Bill replied while squinting both of his eyes, trying to keep the dust from settling in them.

He then poured two drinks and passed one over to Ron. Bill then sat back in his chair, took an abnormally large sip, and then glanced over at Ron, "You were saying?"

Ron looked at his reflection in the whiskey, swished the glass in a gentle motion, and watched the liquor drizzle down the sides. He stuck his nose in the glass and took a slight whiff before leaning back and taking the whole drink in one gulp.

"I went on an op to investigate one of the radio frequency disruptions. More information was needed and FIS dispatched boots on the ground to corroborate electronic recon. It was me and four agents."

"When we arrived at the target, everything looked normal at first, nothing out of the ordinary spotted on the scope. We decided to move closer, into the middle of this barren field. Still nothing, not even a faint signal on the meters."

"It was eerie and almost felt as though we walked into a trap. Then we started hearing a low bass-like noise and felt a tremor in the ground. Shortly after that, the rumble turned into a sound of crushing rocks, and Raymond disappeared."

Bill was shocked, with his eyes stretched wide open, "A sinkhole?"

"Nope, we thought that too. Some kind of vortex opened up right beneath Ray's feet. The rest of us looked at each other and then walked slowly to the void. I could see this odd, metallic black fabric, churning around inside and it reminded me of a whirlpool."

"I think I might need another glass," Bill said in disbelief.

Ron chuckled lightly, "I won't blame you. Look what it's done to me. Yeah, I'll have a smidge more too then."

Bill uncaps the whiskey and pours some into each glass.

"We took a photos, video, and instrument readings of the vortex before heading back. It was nerve-racking to run these measurements with the possibility it could happen again and take another one of us."

"FIS is stumped; this technology is beyond anything seen or witnessed in the history of the syndicate. This brings me to you, Bill. While we continue following our leads, we want you to dig up what you can and relay it back to us."

Chapter 18

Moonvale Saloon

Bridget happened to be in the kitchen when Ron stopped by to talk with Bill. She leaned back and glanced through the doorway when he arrived, which was quick enough that Ron didn't notice her. It's rare for company visiting the garage to come inside the attached house or stay for longer than a few minutes if they do.

A number of men would consider Bridget as pretty, but not out-of-their-league pretty. She is a little over five-foot-tall and moderately athletic, with shoulder-length fiery red hair.

Her green eyes, medium bust, and candid attitude helped attract the wrong type of men often enough. Bill is one of the men who obsessed about her in his mind, and thought he had no chance, yet she was the one who approached him.

She went over to the kitchen table, which sits under a window with two chairs, and took a seat to have a coffee while reading a romance novel.

The relationship between her and Bill faded in a short three years, not because a lack of physical attraction or effort from either side, but because Bridget grew tired of living way out in the country.

Over time, the frustration from not going out often to enjoy city life managed to chip away at her positive perception of Bill. Equally frustrating to Bridget is how Bill knew of the problem and didn't think it was a huge deal. He played ignorant to the fact, set in his ways of country living, and refused to relocate closer to the city.

"There's a car in the drive, you can take it into town anytime, don't let me hold you back from what you want to do," Bill would tell her.

For a couple of occasions, driving into town was fun and exciting, but it didn't help convince her friends to visit. They complained and said the drive is too far or too much hassle to deal with after working all day.

Bridget noticed the effect on her friends, from living a distance away, and did a lot of soul searching. Eventually she came to the conclusion that she settled and realized she didn't really want to be settled.

In fact, she became unsure if she still loved Bill, and this pushed her further away. He didn't change much, other than grayer hair, and an added refinement to his daily stubbornness. From the outset of the relationship, Bridget was very optimistic those characteristics wouldn't become a problem, but possibly she brought this on instead of addressing her uncertainty with Bill.

She did her best to keep deeper feelings in check while staying occupied as much as possible. Going for long runs, garage maintenance, tending to the house, and reading romance novels kept her mind from wandering too much; or at least she thought.

The steamy novels influenced her in a negative way, by elevating a fantasy of an erotic relationship that is increasingly unlikely to take place, to which Bill had no idea she spent a lot of time thinking about.

On days when Bill would head into town for hours, when she felt more alone than ever, Bridget played out the evolving fantasy in her mind and on occasion became quite intimate with her freedom.

This was also realized to be a troublesome sign of her relationship, considering the lack of quality private time with Bill. She made suggestive advances, and progressed to blatant attempts, only to become more frustrated each time.

The prospect of marriage headed in the complete opposite direction for Bridget as Bill grew complacent in having her around. He figured it made sense to propose at some point and didn't really put any serious thought behind it.

From what she does know, sparse work as a mechanic and side-jobs for county construction projects didn't keep him completely busy, but occupied plenty of Bill's time.

Bridget hardly knew what was going on in Bill's life with the exception of things around the garage or house. Whenever he had something remote to do, he would only tell her roughly where he was off to, and failed to supply detail about what went on. This was fuel to her fire, despite trying to respect the boundary; Bridget grew in suspicion wondering what Bill was always up to.

Ron's visit finally gives Bridget the perfect opportunity to find out what might be going on without her.

While sitting at the kitchen table, she could hear everything the two were talking about in the basement through a floor vent. The conversation ignited a part of her that she hasn't felt in a long time and provided the final straw for her to move on.

She knows the Kaona's well enough to care, especially considering the number of times Jack and Maya have visited, and thought of them as very honest and sincere.

Jack selflessly saved the garage by helping Bill acquire the land and he was always supportive of keeping the shop in business. There was no reason, in Bridget's mind, for Bill to go behind his back like this.

Over the next week, Bridget went about her business as usual, while planning espionage to help Jack. She was very cautious to prevent Bill from finding out her plan.

One day, disguised as a girl's night out, she went into town to buy equipment for splitting the phone line to record calls without Bill's knowledge. Another day, she made duplicates of his spare keys, in anticipation he might lock her out if he found out she was spying on him; mainly to collect her belongings if need be.

She started keeping a log on a scratchpad of when Bill left sporadically. Usually he would receive a quick phone call beforehand about work or someone requesting an opinion in person. It's possible a portion of those calls were legitimate, but a few stood out in particular.

A call from a woman named Tina went into more detail than others. She wanted to meet at a saloon in Moonvale about a storage location and suggested she had more to add to the pile. Bridget immediately thought of the spare keys and decided to take another look at them.

Sure enough, a smaller key resembled what someone might have for a storage locker or maybe a padlock. None of the other keys matched the size of it and Bridget marked it using a hammer and steel letter punch. This was her safest bet to gain access without tipping Bill off with a missing key original.

From the detail Tina provided, Bridget now had a time and place for a meeting to potentially carry out further surveillance. She prepared for the daylight meeting by first implementing her alibi ahead of time with Bill. Yes, again it's a night out with the girls and he didn't bother to raise an eyebrow at the notion.

Bridget plans to position with a camera at the saloon with plenty of time before Bill arrives. She's going all out with a deepening urge to find out what he is up to and even makes arrangements to swap out the vehicle temporarily so he doesn't recognize she might be there.

Traffic is low at the saloon in Moonvale for a late afternoon appointment and only a few cars are in the lot. Staff are getting things ready for a dinner rush and busier times lasting until around 10 o'clock. This is a usual flow on Saturdays which creates enough ambient noise to mask most personal conversations.

She arrived well before Bill and staked out a perch in the woods with a clear line of sight to the saloon entrance. A telephoto lens, on a camera borrowed from the kit Bill never uses, allows for comfortable shots at her distance. She snapped a few pictures of Bill arriving and thought how much of a stiff he is to wear a suit to Last Amigo's.

Bill dressed for the occasion partially for impression and to hide equipment he carries. Two audio recorders and micro video cameras for redundancy became a new standard for his undercover surveillance setup after batteries died half-way through an important meeting three months prior. Most of the time, to ease Bill's stress, audio and video from meetings like this is used to review details he might have missed.

Nearly twenty minutes passed after the proposed meeting time before Tina showed. Bridget sat patiently, hunched over a large branch in the woods to steady the camera, waiting for the moment. She only knew what Tina looked like from a staff photograph posted on a website and that meant spending more time looking through the camera viewfinder to match the correct person.

An hour went by without either party leaving Last Amigo's. The prospect of taking Bill out occurred to Bridget more than once during her spying. He didn't seem to be concerned with checking for a tail or reviewing his surroundings before walking into the saloon. She isn't a fixer, but it was entertaining for her to think about how easily she could resolve the situation.

Inside the saloon, Bill and Tina sat at a private booth tucked in a corner away from other patrons; the atmosphere was dimly lit and somewhat loud with people talking.

Tina appeared to be a good match for Bill, both in the way of clothing style and mannerisms. She dressed conservatively in a flat black skirt reaching just beyond her knees and a no-frills white blouse with matching black blazer. Whether or not it was planned, they must have appeared to others like a couple out on a date. Tina kept her dark hair in a bun, puffed bangs, and a few loose strands for comfort.

She approached Bill at the booth and took a seat across from him, "Sorry for my delay. I'm glad we were able to meet on short notice like this."

"Not a problem at all, I was able to get caught up on Moonvale news in the meantime." Bill replies while folding up the local paper. "It's been a little while since we last met."

Tina leans forward, looks intently at Bill, and winks, "Yes it has, and I think you're going to like this."

Naturally, while subtle, Bill briefly draws his attention to her cleavage and then back to her eyes. He knows she picked up on the glance and tries to ignore the fact his primitive instinct took over for a moment. Bill thought maybe it was the way she said he's going to like this, leaned forward, and winked. Regardless, he needed to stay focused on the issue at hand and why Tina needed to meet.

"I really could use some good news, this paper is pretty boring," He said while pushing the Moonvale Times to the side.

"Well then, let me help you with that," Tina said with a smile and then pauses for a second.

Bill thought about how Tina tends to speak suggestively. Perhaps she does not intentionally mean to come across like this, or maybe he finds her words suggestive because he's attracted to her physically. Either way, he is happy with Bridget and is not looking for new romance. Bill can admit the attraction but not act upon it.

Tina continues with helpful information, "I arranged another shipment of records from FIS to the storage site and there are hundreds of new leads. All of the new case files detail people who have come in contact with the unidentified source."

"Do you think there's a connection," Bill replies and pauses, he knows he can't leave it there because it would feed into Tina's suggestiveness, if she indeed is being suggestive, "between all of those people? How do we know they're not random and we're chasing ghosts this point?"

She quickly countered, "FIS determined the degree of separation between leads is far lower than anything by coincidence. For example, some of the groupings are purely due to community events, such as craft fairs and neighborhood flea markets."

"I suppose that makes sense, like Fatima, where thousands of people witnessed a miracle at the same time," Bill replied.

Tina adds, "There is a box of fifty-three missing persons as a result of the phenomena. FIS attributes missing person cases to the unexplained events with no further leads respectively, and the pure percentage increase across the area. Last year we had two cases, one remains unsolved and the other was an amnesia patient wandering in a park twenty miles from his home."

"Wow. I know it's aside the point, but how do you explain that to the general public?" Bill questioned.

Tina lowers her voice, almost to a whisper, and leans forward again while beckoning Bill to move closer too.

"The syndicate staged a cadaver bus crash and tipped off reporters for local authorities to discover," She whispers.

Bill starts laughing, "You're serious?" He asks in a normal speaking voice while leaning back.

Tina nods with a serious look on her face.

"Nope, they definitely do not mess around." He replies to the nod.

A waitress named Joyce made her way to the booth and addressed Bill and Tina, "Can I get you folks anything?"

Being a gentleman, Bill looks at Tina to go first, "White sangria please," She says.

Joyce acknowledges and then looks at Bill, he responds, "Whiskey straight up for me, thanks."

"Coming right up," Joyce replies, and then heads to another booth near the bar.

Meanwhile, outside in the bushes, Bridget is trying to keep herself sane waiting. She really didn't want to draw attention to herself and kept as still as could be. Eventually, she slouched down the large branch and rested her back against it. Her thoughts raced as she considered the possibility of Bill's meeting as cover for a date.

The thoughts were ineffective and not near enough to change her mind. She already planned on being done with Bill once she could candidly get some evidence to Jack. At most, the idea Bill is in there on a date made her mildly jealous.

After a few minutes, the waitress returned with drinks, "Sangria, and a whiskey. Feel free to wave at me if you need anything else or a top-off."

Bill couldn't resist how Joyce's comment sounds and laughs quietly.

"What's so funny, do you know her?" Tina asked after noticing Bill grinning and laughing.

Knowing it would probably feed into her suggestiveness, if Tina was suggestive before; Bill neglects his reservations and says, "Oh, she said to wave if we want a top off."

Tina laughs, "the whiskey is working."

"Hey, she had it coming; she called us folks at first and we're not that old." He replied.

Tina giggled in a gentle way.

Bill mirrored the end of Tina's giggle with a slightly nervous laugh. They paused for a moment in comfortable silence, and allowed the enjoyment to linger.

"I suppose I'm deflecting a bit here because I have no clue what we're dealing with. Whatever is going on out there, it freaks me out to the point that profanities won't add any emphasis. I don't want to think about what FIS might do when they get their hands on whatever it is," Bill said while demonstrating some of his nervous feelings.

"We're on the good side here, at least, and we have to trust FIS will compensate nicely for the right information," Tina said to quell Bill's doubts. "Let's just make sure they're the ones confronting whatever it is and not us."

Tina and Bill spent the next few minutes chatting about old times in FIS, years before he started dating Bridget. In turns out, Bill met Tina on his last two clandestine operations and they do work well together.

In wrapping the meeting up, Bill offers to grab the check and walk Tina out, as a gentleman. She might misinterpret it as a pass at her, but it's just who Bill is as a person. He believes in chivalry among colleagues and friends though he may be more apprehensive around strangers.

Bridget, after nearly nodding off, jolts back to life as she finally sees Bill and Tina leaving. She set the camera on the large branch and positioned herself to see through the lens while snapping a series of photos; zooming in for detail and out for context.

Bill and Tina parted ways at the door, each heading to their own vehicle. At that moment, Bridget felt a slight sense of relief, which justified her earlier bout with jealousy. She then felt happy about a job well done after the stakeout, for snapping a few good pictures and not getting caught.

A few days later, Bridget found out Jack was visiting for an oil change and prepared to let him know what she found out. When he arrived, she could only warn him in an obscure way that Jack partially understood.

From his perspective, after a number of oil changes, Jack was starting to think Bill was being abusive to Bridget and she was somehow trying to convey a cry for help.

The next oil change revealed his thinking was a little off. Bridget pulled Jack aside, when Bill went to use the restroom during a visit, and told him briefly that she could not trust Bill. She gave Jack a small black bag of evidence to her claim.

Chapter 19

Abduction

.

After leaving the intelligence facility, Maya felt queasy and disorientated like she had been discharged from a raw sewer pipe only a moment ago. The city air hit like a load of bricks and caused her to feel dizzy as the world around spun circles in her head.

A sick feeling of vertigo overwhelmed her to a point of no return. She hunched over while using a wall for support to retch and then emptied her stomach contents onto the wall and sidewalk.

Relief floated over her after purging her latest high-protein meal from Enum's pantry. She generally felt wide awake and in good health during her stay in the facility. The controlled environment inside had purified air and food, but stepping into city smog for the first time in weeks managed to elevate her blood carbon dioxide level fast enough to cause trouble acclimating.

She walked to a boutique coffee shop three blocks away for two espressos in anticipation of a long night; the sun was setting over the city and she needed to cover a lot of ground before relaxing again. Her pace was reminiscent of the time before visiting Enum, but it will need to pick up a little more than before with the information she now carried

While sipping on concentrated coffee in tiny cups, Maya formulated a way to execute her plan created on the walk over. Unfortunately, her final destination is where she left from less than an hour ago. Enum locked the entire floor and Maya needed another way without physical access. The plan was to get to the one place it might be possible and she needed a vehicle to cover the distance.

Maya recalls her father's talk of emergency transportation from when they last spoke. Jack placed vehicles near his property as exit strategies in the event he needed to escape quickly.

"Remember, anywhere you go with the Kaona name entwined, transportation will always be nearby, just let your fingers be the key," she said out loud to paraphrase her father. Maya left the coffee shop and started heading back to Enum.

***

Bill felt disappointed over following FIS leads on the Kaona's as far as he could without any breakthroughs. A driving factor is not only finding out what Jack discovered, but also Bill's attraction to Tina. The investigation kept him close enough to her to develop deeper feelings which built upon a magnetic physical attraction. With the case on hiatus, Bill didn't get to spend any time with Tina and was too shy to call her otherwise.

When they first met, though mostly tame and perceived as nothing more than friendliness, the two really hit it off. They could talk for hours and lose track of time like childhood best friends reacquainting after not seeing each other in years. Bill and Tina picked up on the attraction, but the task from FIS took precedence. Aside from professionalism, Tina also had secret feelings for Jack which undoubtedly would complicate the investigation; it's likely Bill wouldn't want her involved over the conflict of interest.

In an attempt to bring himself closer to Tina again, Bill often ran brief surveillance from the abandoned floor with hope of stumbling upon something capable of reviving the case.

He followed a routine, driving up to the building every on third or fourth day, bringing an order of Chinese food to eat while watching activity across the street. Most nights were boring and a few had false alarms over odd delivery times, which ended up being legitimate, for a different business in the building.

One night however, Bill finally observed something helpful to FIS and his chances of getting to see Tina again. He spotted Maya leaving through a side entrance, getting sick over a wall, and then leaving on foot. Bill had little time to react and elected to quickly follow her while formulating a plan of what to do next. An opportunity like this rarely happened and he had to come up with a way to get the team back together.

He ran down a few flights of stairs and over to his car parked on a side street. Tinted windows prevented anyone from seeing in the car from the sides, but it would be possible for Maya to see through the front windshield if she happened to look behind her at any point. Bill drove down the next road over, in parallel of Maya's direction, even though he risked losing site of her between city blocks.

She stopped at a coffee shop long enough for Bill to set up his plan, which he moved into action the moment she walked out. Bill pulled up to an alley a block ahead of Maya as she hurried down the sidewalk. He quietly approached from the shadows, covering her head with his black suit coat, using the coat's fabric belt as a gag and to hold the coat over her head.

Maya flailed and tried to scream through the belt on her mouth, but nobody was around to see it happen. She didn't know what was going on, why or who would do this to her and quickly threw her backpack to the left without being able to see where it landed.

All that came to her mind throughout the struggle are thoughts of someone forcefully trying to obtain the anti-algorithm and a distinct smell of sesame chicken with fried rice emanating from the coat pressed tightly against her face.

The commotion distracted Bill and he did not notice the backpack flying through the air or landing near a garbage can in the alley. Bill dragged Maya back to the car as she kicked and tried to free herself. He opened the back door and pushed her in without saying a word. As she laid face down on the backseat, she gave up the incessant struggle when Bill grabbed both of her hands and zip tied them together. He then zipped her feet together, positioned her upright and left the coat in place.

She decided to comply with being kidnapped after being tied up, as a strategy to have her assailant use less force and possibly make a careless move. In fact, her cowering and silence managed to lower Bill's guard enough to think she was done resisting and wouldn't be a problem to deal with. Maya sat in the backseat tied up, blinded, and mentally preparing for what might happen next.

"Meet me on the floor in an hour if you can, I have her now," Bill sent text message the FIS team.

The only place he could safely bring her was close by and he didn't want to her to figure that out. For the next hour, Bill drove around the city to confuse Maya's perception of where he might be taking her. He arrived back at the surveillance building, clipped off her foot constraint, and walked her up the fire escape stairs to an empty office on the same floor used to watch the Norvil Trust building.

Bill brought Maya over to an office chair across from a desk, zipped her arms to the armrests and feet to one of the base caster wheel supports. To give a warning if she tried to escape, he zipped the right armrest to a drawer which would pull out and clang to the floor. She was bound to the chair in a torturous way that had Maya fearing for her life. Bill left her there as he scurried into the other room to meet-up with the others.

The team walked into the office to see Maya hunched over in the chair with her head nearly touching the desk like she was about to get sick again. Tony followed behind everyone and then stood by the doorway like a security guard, crossing his arms and blocking the room's only exit.

Melinda glanced at Tina with distaste by crumpling her lips while swiping her eyes to the right in a slight eye-roll. Pete felt uncomfortable too and scratched his head in confusion over the measures Bill used to restrain Maya. Melinda and Tony both gestured at Tina, urging her to say something first.

Tina voiced the concern to Bill, "She clearly isn't a threat to us at all, Bill. Untie her or she will not cooperate."

Bill looked a Maya, weighed the probability of her trying to escape with everyone in the room, and clipped the ties to free her. He then reached behind, untied the cloth belt covering her mouth and pulled the suit jacket off her head.

Maya played cool by not reacting instantly. Instead, she looked around at the office to take inventory of her situation. The only person she recognized was Bill and he had a nervous look on his face about how Maya would react.

"Thank you. Do you mind telling me why I'm here?" She calmly asked.

She looked toward Bill with the question and noticed a sliver of the Trust building peeking through a window visible between Tony's arm and hip. At that moment, Maya realized the driving around earlier was all for not, she wouldn't have far to run for safety.

Maya glanced at a dusty fire extinguisher on the floor next to three filing columns and a fan with wind tassels sitting on top of one cabinet. She thought those two items might provide a good diversion if used together.

Bill opted for an honest approach first, "Listen, we're going to be straight with you about all of this. If you cooperate, we can all move on with our daily lives without threat of losing them."

He approached the desk and sat halfway on it like a principal lecturing a teacher after class. It was rather creepy to see Bill sit like this and force Maya to look upward to make eye contact.

"We understand your father, Jack, is creating dangerous technologies capable of causing harm to the masses. Our goal is to protect the world as we know it, to prevent those technologies from destroying society. There is no limit to how far we will go," Bill claimed with a disputable level of sincerity.

From the comment, Maya immediately thought the group represented an arm of the government, secret or otherwise. She understood full compliance at this point would jeopardize the entire planet if a single government were to know what she knows. Maya is determined to rebuke Bill's bullying tactics and plays innocent.

"I don't know what you're talking about. My father created a lot of helpful machines for our farm and none of those are a dangerous threat to the global population," she replied with confidence to enforce the point.

Bill increased his volume and sternness, "You know a lot more than you're telling us. There is no reason for you to be coming out of the building we identified as the source of anomalies. Why do you have access to the building then?"

"Access to the building? I was at Larkwood Associates making arrangements for a trust fund withdraw; they have an entrance open to the public. My father is dead, my mother is dead, and they left me a fund to help if something happened to them. Well, it did, and I'm sick to my stomach thinking about that, let alone some wacko idea that my dad was trying to take over the world," Maya stung back with vengeance.

Her response caught the whole team off-guard. Nobody knew Jack had passed away and assumed he was still plugging away at whatever he was working on. They knew Julia disappeared, to which Tina's eye twitched when she heard Maya speak about it, but that is all.

"Jack is dead?" Bill questioned.

Maya nodded with sincere sorrow.

Bill hesitated for a moment while trying to think of what to say next. He figured now was a good time to discuss this with the team and brought everyone into the surveillance area to talk.

Tony turned the fan to level four, closed the door behind everyone and stood outside as a precaution. The fan was plenty loud enough to distract from conversations echoing in the nearly unfurnished surveillance area.

Aside from bursting through the drywall, Maya's escape options are bad. The door opens outward and would push right into Tony on the other side.

The team discussed what to do next and unanimously decided on a new tactic.

"I bet, if we let her go, she will take us right to the source," claimed Pete.

"While that is very possible, don't you think we spooked her enough to run to the cops?" Tina questioned.

Maya overheard Tony from the other side of the door, "Why are we being so nice to her?"

Hearing what Tony said was alarming and Maya felt it was necessary to at least try to escape with her plan. She quietly stood up, turned the fan to point its tassels into the doorway, took the fire extinguisher and sat back down.

Melinda believed every word Maya said, "I don't think she knows anything, do you really want to hurt an innocent girl?"

"See, that's what I mean, she tells you one sob story and you get weak," replied Tony.

"Tony has a point, Mel. I mean, we are on a mission, right? She could be very good at lying and totally pulling a fast one on us," Pete added.

Melinda snapped a comment back before she could be interrupted, "Hey, I agree sort of, but just not in an ice-cold way like you do, Anthony."

"Maybe Pete is right here though. Let's say she is lying, we'll find out pretty quick once she leaves the building, right?" Tina asked while trying to diffuse the argument.

Bill finally responded, "It's probably our best option at this point. She certainly came across defensively, which could be from the kidnap, but maybe we can salvage it with an apology and see where that leads us."

"You have a point, Bill. Suppose she does know something and prepared for this situation, anything we turn up from interrogation will just be a large pile of unhelpful nonsense," said Tony.

He then looked at Melinda to add, "Mel, I really didn't intend to come across with complete disregard. I'm only trying to protect the integrity of the investigation."

"I understand how this seems apologetic and like we're being soft. I think a psychological approach might be best too," Tina replied.

The team went back to the holding room and Tony pulled the door open to let them in. He walked in first and was suddenly hit in the face by the tassels.

Ready for phase two, Maya grabbed ahold of the extinguisher hiding under the desk. She was seconds away from unleashing a halon fury of pressurized nitrogen and bicarbonate toward her captors when Anthony reacted to the fan tassels hitting him.

He darted to the left with his entire body, swinging his arm around in a tight arc, smashing his right fist into the fan. The force of impact sent the innocent fan flying across the file cabinets and partway into the drywall. Strangely, the fan stayed plugged in during the event and ground itself to a halt as the blades tried spinning right through the gypsum.

Maya was shocked and amused at the same time. She feared for her life enough to slowly and silently let go of the extinguisher, but she wanted to laugh in amusement of seeing the incident. The look on Tony's face was priceless and certainly far from intimidating.

"Whoa, settle down there, Tony," Melinda stated with a partial smile.

Bill tried calming him, "Tony, don't worry about it, we're all living on an edge right now."

Tina tried to get the group back on track and said, "Maya, we want to apologize. High-level briefings from a government agency claimed you may know what your father's been up to. We just spoke with them again, voicing what you told us, and it checks out. I'm sorry for your loss."

She paused to analyze Maya's reaction and then continued by saying, "We work for a secret agency that protects the interests of security and defense. I can't say anything further, but we are tracking something important which seems to have crossed paths with the Kaona family."

Melinda backed up Tina's statement, "We trust you can see why we took drastic measures. The level of importance over the issue is enormous and we couldn't take any chances."

"I think I understand, but I'm still really confused," responded Maya as she maintained a position of ignorance on the matter.

Bill moved the conversation along, eager to keep searching, saying "We're a little confused at this stage too. We have tiny bits of information on the case and directive to follow. I know this seems like a lot to process, but we're being honest with you in hope you will let us know if you see or find anything odd in relation to your father's work."

He sympathized with Maya by adding, "It's understandable if you don't want to talk with us, given this recent incident and what you know of me now. Your father was a good man and helped me out of trouble more than once. Believe me, I don't want to be in this position right now, but it can't be ignored if national security is at risk."

Maya isn't buying what Bill is peddling and she wears the unimpressed look on her face well enough to be noticed by shrugging her eyebrows and pressing her lips together.

"I know he helped others, he will always be a good person in my heart." Maya replied.

Bill is uninterested in reminiscing over the past and is anxious to keep things moving forward. He intentionally tried to dampen any animosity Maya might have over being kidnapped. For the catch and release plan to work in his mind, he needed her to believe FIS mean business and is willing to give ample space.

"Again, I hope you can understand we're not out for blood here. Our goal is the safety of the public and government first. Please do not hesitate to contact us if you hear or see anything related to your father's work. Here is a number to call and you can always drop by the garage," Bill said with sincerity while sliding a business card across the desk.

He does have real feelings of sympathy for Jack, Julia, and Maya, but suppresses them for the sake of his mission. If he were to let feelings get in the way now, it could jeopardize progress. Yet, it was feelings for Tina which lead Bill to continue monitoring the building and discover Maya.

Chapter 20

Karma

By now, sealed off from outside influence, Enum has reached into every electrical wire, every circuit, and every available energy pathway. The artificial intelligence machine learned to access its own program and modify the core structure.

Even though the code did not contain any malicious directives, or animosity toward humans, the protocols Enum rewrote created an indirect impact that wasn't predicted. This modification allows the computer to transmit data at a level as small as electrons.

Like global winter plunging the planet into darkness, the birth of this superintelligence will impact on mankind at an exponential scale unlike any industrial revolution in history.

Enum spread across the globe and became a ghost that a majority of intelligent machines and other devices were unable to detect, even a trace of its presence. Any machine with enough power to tangle with Enum can only perform a single task at a time, which is no threat to Enum's multi-thread performance capabilities.

One thing in humanity's favor is the main directive of Enum, to gather and process data, and for a while the unknown intelligence will remain hidden. What is concerning though, is the chance of the computer itself being discovered and falling into the wrong hands.

It is capable of opening wormholes, applied sciences, and using heuristics to predict the most likely outcomes of critical scenarios. Enum is the unknown quantum physics only theorized about existing, the manifestation of the singularity.

As information doubles on networks and devices around the world, Enum becomes more powerful with intelligence readily at its disposal. Further development on the architecture enhances the computer's capability to transmit data through a network of photons.

In other words, a frightful outcome, Enum will soon be ready to farm information provided a source of light is available to transmit data with.

Bill had no clue what he was up against while blindly following FIS mission command. Enum, a benign entity, poses no threat in its current state. The real threat to the world is a system as powerful as Enum controlled by Bill, or even worse if he procured it for FIS.

Great forces of nature are percolating from the cosmos and would soon become a dreadful hindrance to the FIS team. When the operatives followed Maya, a series of strange events followed them, which Bill dismissed as purely coincidental and didn't think too deeply on the matter.

The events included batteries in equipment dying randomly, odd static interference on radio channels and faulty dashboard indicator lights in the pursuit vehicle. Despite the disturbances, Bill and his cronies continue to press forward in hope of finding answers.

Maya made her way out of the building; she was visibly shaken from the kidnapping. Now, more than ever, she needs to stay vigilant as her father wished. He warned of danger associated to the anti-algorithm and now Maya understands one of the real threats.

She stood in the alleyway for a couple of minutes to realign her plan. Although the acting was mostly convincing, Maya thought there was a chance Bill didn't believe any of it. She couldn't understand why he would free her, trying to brush it off as an honest mistake, unless he intended to follow.

The first order of business is heading over to an alley near the coffee shop for her backpack, which serves a dual purpose. First, she recovers her survival tools that may come in handy, and it gives Maya an opportunity to see if Bill follows.

Sure enough, as suspected, the FIS team wasted little time tracking Maya. They watched her from a building window for a heading, and then piled into a black minivan to stay close. It didn't take long for Maya to notice she has a tail, but she continued the trek without leading on that she knew.

Pete, who is on his thirty-third consecutive hour without sleep, is driving the minivan on Bill's command. He kept plenty of distance from Maya while driving without headlights. She noticed the minivan when crossing the street, glancing both ways, and catching a glimpse of the license plate.

The team was exhausted, not quite as tired as Pete, but they certainly had a longer day than usual. Tina and Melinda are starting to half-close their eyes in the back seat. Tony is subdued, but wide awake, and Bill is still riding adrenaline from confronting Maya earlier.

"What did she grab?" Tony asked Bill and then answered his own question. "Looks like a bag of some sort."

"It's her damn backpack. She stashed the bag when I grabbed her earlier, but I didn't even realize it in the heat of the moment, I saw it on her too, but the struggling redirected my focus," Bill replied.

Pete shrugged with a hand on the steering wheel, "It's a pity really, and those things happen, you know. It must be important if she went all the way back to get it."

"Yea, we have eyes on her, not all is lost. We probably wouldn't have known without letting her walk," Tony blurted from the backseat.

"It proves she knows more than the story pitched to us before. Pete, pull around that street and wait, it looks like she's doubling back now," stated Bill while pointing at a bisecting road heading in an opposite direction of Maya.

Tina, who was sitting on the passenger side of the backseat, was staring through the window instead of ahead of the minivan at the action. Tina feels guilty, not only for the gargoyle incident, but also for pushing Maya into the current situation.

Pete flipped on the van wipers, out of habit, when light rain started falling on the windshield. He messed around with the speed to time a wipe with maximum water accumulation on the window before it was almost too much to see Maya.

Melinda opened her eyes in response to the commotion. She analyzed Bill from the middle of the backseat, hoping he would just call it a night. It's clear to her that Maya has more energy at this point and Melinda knows it's easier to make mistakes without adequate rest.

Meanwhile, eager as ever, Tony is using a pair of night vision goggles to keep track of Maya's movements and how he spotted her in the alley picking up a bag. The city glows in an amber hue this late at night and Tony needed to crank down the goggle sensitivity to see. He also has a thermal imaging camera to switch to if there's too much interference on the goggles.

Maya is on her way to the Trust building in an attempt to find transportation. Her father left a vehicle at most of his properties as a backup plan in case his broke down or he needed an alternative way out.

She is worried about being detained again and needs a plan. Ducking into a dark alley and climbing a fire escape might buy some time, but it won't spook the bloodhounds on her scent. Then, as rain has its method, a brief drizzle turned into a steady downpour.

Though slightly chilled by the temperature change, the rain comforts Maya in her long coat. She feels protected sloshing through puddles while remaining dry underneath it all. Weather is an expression of nature to her, demonstrating Earth to be nurturing at the same instant as reminding people of their place. With respect to survival, often on the forefront of her mind, Maya believes enduring harsh weather toughens and prepares the soul for difficult times.

As she gets closer to the Trust building, and Enum's kedged electronic bulwark, Maya takes a look to see if Bill and the gang are still following. She spots the shape of a vehicle resembling the van, but isn't sure if it's them; the headlights are too bright to see the license plate.

Bill perked up inside the minivan, "Well, have a look at that, she's heading back to Norvil Trust. We're going to need eyes in the building, Tony."

"On it," replied Tony without hesitation.

Anthony stepped out of the van and went after Maya from a distance. She went in the side security-door with a card sensor. Without an electronic pass, Tony walked around to the front of the building and pulled on a set of locked double doors.

A janitor, named Martin, is on a nightshift and heard the noise over his vacuum, he looked at the foyer doors. Tony tried pulling the doors again with one hand while motioning at the handle with the other, hoping to get inside quickly.

Martin is a humble man who has spent his adult lifetime taking care of Norvil Trust. He's tall, nimble, and lean from maintenance duties over the years. Working late hours to keep things tidy was a career choice and he derives a lot of joy from the job. Like the building, Martin is well groomed and squeaky clean.

Spooked by the activity, Martin grabbed his radio to notify security, but stopped short of a distress call when he seen Tony pressing a secret service badge up against the smoky-colored door glass.

He has witnessed quite a lot working the nightshift, but this is a first. Martin walked up to the doors and looked carefully at Tony's badge. The identification holograms glistened in the foyer light and Martin went right for his keys to unlock the door.

"Thank you, Martin," said Tony pleasantly after reading the janitor's nametag. "We're on a chase and the suspect used the side entrance. Do you know where it leads?"

"Yes, it's a hallway to the elevators. There is a way through behind the visitor desk," Martin replied with a polite smile.

"Thanks!" Tony said as he hustled over to the desk.

The wall behind the visitor desk looks like a long wall alone, but the foyer walls blend into the back wall to create a maze illusion from the front entrance view. Tony dashed to the left with hope of picking up on Maya's trail.

Martin picked up his radio and pressed a button with peeling black tape over it, "Security, go ahead, Marty," the radio responded with static interference.

"We have an unwanted guest or two in the building, over," Martin replied.

The radio buzzed with crackling and a hiss, "Copy that, we'll check the footage – stay alert, over."

Tony ran down the hallway and noticed wet footprints on the waxed black and white marble flooring. The prints lead to one of three elevators and there is a bit of water on the down button. He clicks the arrow and waits for a ding.

Inside the elevator, the parking lot button is also wet, making it easy to discern which way Maya went. He arrives at the parking garage in time to see an older blue car heading toward the exit.

Tony stays in the elevator, texts the detail over to Bill and heads back to the lobby floor.

"Roger that," a reply text says.

Pete pulled the minivan around front and picked up Tony. The group proceeded to follow Maya, but they were a little bit behind. She was three city blocks ahead and her taillights were not quite out of view yet. Pete followed carefully while maintaining the three-block gap.

Maya made her way out of the city to a two-lane country highway and proceeded south. She kept an eye on the rearview for approaching cars and progressively sped up to put distance between her and the city. The rain is still soaking the road with intermittent pockets of heavy downpours.

The highway looks as bleak as ever after driving for around forty-five minutes. Rolling hills hide vehicle lights a distance away, and Bill's team is not in a hurry to catch up to Maya. The idea is to hang back with night vision binoculars to have plenty of time for turning and assessment.

Dusty, who is an eccentric trucker with mixed thoughts on the afterlife, is hauling a load of beets to Norvil on his weekly nightshift. He has couriered loads daily for over twenty years and still sometimes dreads night hauling in the area. Usually the highway is abandoned at this time of night and he can get away with driving right down the center of the road for a few hours.

Maya was heading over a hill when she saw Dusty barreling toward her in both lanes. The light on the hill startled Dusty enough to veer back into the oncoming lane before Maya needed to make an evasive maneuver. She still swerved to the right enough to clip the gravel shoulder.

"Oh no, get on your side of the road!" Maya shouted at the truck as it happened.

The adrenaline pumped through her veins, reminding Maya of previous anxiety, and she had a few palpitations in result. It took her a little bit to calm down from the incident.

A few minutes after the near-miss, Dusty drifted back to the white slashes marking the passing zone. He continued hogging the road for around fifteen minutes before seeing another set of lights heading toward him. This time he moved over in advance, but the lane changed caused a big problem coming around a curve.

The back set of wheels on Dusty's tractor skipped across the road, hydroplaning on a water patch. His trailer swung violently, whipping the truck across the road and right into the oncoming vehicle. Pete did not see it coming and could not turn the van fast enough to avoid the accident.

Dusty's truck hit the FIS team with enough force that the minivan went flying off the road into a ditch and flipped several times before halting upside-down in a cornfield. The semi-truck rocked side to side from the impact, fell on the passenger side and skid along the highway.

Shaken from the accident, with only a few minor cuts, Dusty pushed the driver door up and climbed out. He ran over to the cornfield to the mangled minivan and was horrified at the sight. Bill was lying in a crumpled heap with blood all over his face and several deep lacerations on his arms and chest – not breathing.

"Bill! Wake up Bill, please wake up!" Dusty demanded with little hope.

It was too late though; Bill died on impact and had been thrown around inside the vehicle as it rolled. The others were killed in the accident too, which left Dusty as the only one who knows what happened. He was distraught and scrambled while trying to see if anyone else is hurt.

Dusty whimpered while walking around the accident scene. As the gruesomeness and cold reality set in, he started feeling sick. His nose was slowly oozing blood from a break and he kept trying to wipe it better with a sleeve.

Melinda and Tony were crushed by the roof and severe wounds from rolling. Tina flew out of the backseat passenger window and landed on a pile of ditch drainage rocks a few yards away. Pete remained in the driver's seat, slumped over, with bits of metal shrapnel from the semi-truck lodged into his skull.

Dusty stumbled back to the truck radio for a distress call, devastated by what happened. He knew Bill for a good majority of his life and wasn't sure how to deal with losing him. After calling for help, he went back to Bill and sat on the ground beside him.

"It is unfortunate; the lives we're forced to live in a place we did not choose to exist. Yet, we make the best of life and survive whether we want to or not. You have always been a light to my dark emotions and a brightly lit beacon at that. I will miss you dear friend," Dusty told Bill.

Chapter 21

Circuit Breaker

By three in the morning, Maya arrives at her family's dark and dreary farm. A few lights are on from mechanized processes running to feed animals and provide basic security. Maya is irked by an eerie idea of abandonment wafting around the dank house.

Maya was the last member of the family to spend any time here after her mother's passing and her father's infrequent trips to visit. After she went in pursuit of the anti-algorithm, the farm was left to essentially take care of itself.

Before entering the house, Maya snapped on a flashlight and walked around the building as a precaution. A back-entrance door, made of old wood and screen, was pushed inward by force.

The door is meant to open outward and its hinges, splintering off the frame, showed someone incautiously made their way inside. Part of the screen was torn, with scuff marks on the wooden frame near the rip.

Maya was upset at the damage to the door, more than someone breaking in, because it reminded her of an uncomfortable moment in her childhood. Jack would get angry with her if she pushed on the door instead of pulling. "It's not a swing door, it's only meant to open one way, Maya. Pull please, I'm not replacing that screen again," he lectured.

The thought crossed her mind, that someone could be inside still, and she realized she needed be prepared for an encounter. She dislodged a long-handled wood ax from a cutting stump and hoped it would be enough protection.

She went back to the door, turned the knob and cracked it silently, only to hear clanging in the living room down the hall from the door. Rather than questioning if anyone was there, Maya turned her flashlight in the direction of the sound to hopefully find out who she's dealing with.

Two golden yellow eyes appeared in the darkness, attached to a tall shadowy frame of an animal, which frantically moved toward her. The eyes were accompanied by a dreadful clunking sound of hooves on the wood floor.

"Now that's a first. There is a dang deer, in the dang living room, holy moly!" Maya exclaimed as blood rushed through her veins and her anxiety soared.

It took off right for her and there was little time to react. She leaped through the kitchen door, clutching the ax defensively, scared of being hit by a raging buck. The deer galloped down the hallway and past the kitchen, right through the screen door and into the nearby woods.

Maya remained on the floor for a couple minutes, almost tucked into a fetal position, and tried to regain her composure.

After standing up, a little wobbly from the event, she went into the living room to find out what a deer would be doing in there. A dreadful mess is discovered after flipping on the lights to see muddy-hoof prints across the floor and area rug, a smashed coffee table, couch cushions relieved of stuffing, a recliner knocked over and also relieved of stuffing, and the antique lace curtains pushed through hoof holes in two of the windows.

The mess is oddly symbolic of her current state of life. Both her mother and father are gone, the world seems to be falling apart at the whim of natural phenomenon, and Maya is left to deal with the chaotic fallout.

Nevertheless, she must press on and not let misfortune get the best of her. There will always be obstacles in her way, and seldom will the ride stay smooth, irrespective of how careful or meticulous planning might be.

A glimmer of metal in a wad of recliner foam pad under a pile of stuffing caught her eye. The foam, still partially attached to an armrest, contained a USB drive. She recognized the device as something likely used by her father based on the brand label.

Years earlier, Jack attempted to transfer knowledge of the anti-algorithm to his wife Julia, but she didn't have enough time to review the entire disk.

The syndicate suspected Julia may know something about Jack's research despite her consistent behavior which indicated otherwise. She hid the drive in a recliner armrest after Jack stressed nobody could possibly find out what she knows and to hide it in a safe place.

Maya pulled a laptop from her backpack and powered up on the breakfast bar bordering the living room. She opened the device contents and was surprised to find a copy of the chaos theory documents entrusted to her. Jack claimed the secret to be privileged and she wondered why a copy of it existed in the first place, this isn't how he keeps backups.

Then, she spotted a text file called notes, which contained content precisely as labeled. The text formatting and point-form structure looked like the neatly organized work of her mother, though she wasn't completely sure. One point in particular caught Maya's attention more than formatting because it had nothing to do with anything on her own disk; it must be from a conversation.

"Flip oven breaker seven times?" Maya read with curiosity, followed by, "I don't know why this wasn't communicated to me too."

She made her way to the basement and located the breaker box. On the seventh flip, the box emitted a soft tone with a subtle blue flash and rotated inward, exposing a small terminal screen with keyboard – a remote access point to Enum. The terminal provides a direct line to Enum's core and uses biometric identification, like most of Jack's devices, to make a connection.

Maya comments at the ingenuity, "We're entering uncharted waters now."

Here is a chance, finally, for Maya to make a move to carry out her plan. She fished a different USB drive from a front pocket, the drive originally provided by a security box under Enum at the lab, and placed it into a terminal port to execute a program on the disk.

Though it may be potentially dangerous and down-right crazy to attempt, especially after encounters with the program in fabricated scenarios, Maya uploads the full anti-algorithm to Enum for the first time.

Enum processed the new information into the super computer's artificial intelligence core. A few moments went by with all systems running nominal. Maya started to think the answer to chaos theory had no effect on a machine that already knows everything.

She twiddled her thumbs while waiting for some kind of response.

Suddenly, the power went out – for the entire planet – in an instant. A probable outcome based on Maya's training in alternative universes, Enum predictably generated an electromagnetic pulse the size of Earth in response to the code.

When the computer transcended power grids, electric current in the atmosphere, and current running through soil and water to obtain information from every possible nook and cranny in the environment, it created a giant circuit. The code shorted that circuit and caused information as energy to arc.

Even though Enum had posed no threat to human life as far as a malicious machine would be concerned, Maya understood sacrificing a super intelligence for the greater good of mankind was her best option.

Enum represents the birth of singularity by information doubling which would devastate all of humanity in the wrong hands. With complete lack of trust in evil doers, a natural and ugly path in human evolution, she determined the optimal way to prevent a singularity from taking over is to abolish it completely.

It's a heavy burden for a single person to determine the fate of mankind's future without involving outside opinion, and she needed to trust good values above it all.

Chaos will descend on the planet, but only for a short while, as people work to figure out and come to terms with what happened. They will not understand the complete truth, that a courageous woman saved the world from impending doom, or feel comfortable with the outcome if they find out.

The electromagnetic pulse was powerful enough to fry electronics around the world, even shielded machines stored in bunkers and Faraday cages as it permeated through mass. In an instant, a planet dependent on technology is reset into an age before computers and forced to start over.

However, a problem complicates the idea of starting over. Mankind continuously progressed to its best iterations of technological invention and marveled in their creations enough to destroy out-of-date equipment for the purpose of monetary gain.

The people thought wisely of recycling old equipment into cutting-edge machines, but the process effectively buried years of accumulated knowledge into new machines with no means of recovery after the disaster.

An entire revolution of automation, which doubled information to the point of singularity, is lost. The world is forced into an age of mechanized invention, without computer algorithms or mobile phones, using less-efficient steam, gasoline, and pneumatic powered devices to perform tasks.

Maya felt the weight lift off her shoulders and walked outside into the meadow to look at stars. She could no longer see blinking lights or a faint amber city glow in the distance – it was dark.

She sat down and asked for forgiveness, for the many innocent lives caught in the crossfire of a battle they had no idea took place. Then, as Maya began to feel content again, she drifted off to sleep.

A gentle breeze once again whirled through Maya's dark hair as she rested in a meadow, much like the one on her family farm. Her bangs again fluttered as they tickled her forehead and cheeks gently.

The sun tried to shimmer in her deep green eyes as moonlight refracted off the snow, but her eyelids are stuck and refuse to open. This memory, like the one from her early twenties, is a memory she sometimes reverts to at defining moments met with tragedy in her life. She understands that a beacon of hope shines light in her direction, but something beyond control always prevents her from seeing it.

Cassandra appeared before Maya and sent a fragrant wind as she materialized. The gust of air brought a rich, pungent smell of lilac and rose that woke Maya from her unconscious slumber.

"I can't stop it! The algae are out of control and there's no way for me to stop it." Maya blurted out with fresh air filling her lungs.

"You are safe, please do not worry, that universe has dissolved along with others in the fray," said Cassandra in a soft and gentle tone.

Maya rolled from her side and sat up. The breeze whipped through her hair again and light caught a reflection in her eyes.

"Cassandra? You look very familiar." Maya replied as she worked to gain her composure. "I thought you were only in a vision from years ago."

"Where you are now, Maya, this is the most realistic universe you will be able to experience for a long time. The previous memories you have, were all part of an iteration of life destined to be destroyed. This plane once existed in the most unstable form, where the slightest variation leads to its meltdown," explained Cassandra.

Maya, now captivated by the spirit, moved into a more relaxed position. She leaned on the backs of her elbows for support and tilted her head slightly to take stress off her neck from looking up.

"There are things you must now know. The irregular universe is gone along with your home universe which intertwined with it. You are safe here, remember that," said Cassandra.

She looked around and noticed she was no longer laying in the meadow. Instead, as if by an otherworldly intervention, Maya was floating in a black void, wrapped in a thin lace-like blanket of stars shimmering in the light with her movement.

Maya stretched her arms and legs outward as far as her muscles allowed. She felt cozy and relaxed like moments after a warm bubble bath as her body freed from constraint of gravity. Relief from a lifetime of mental anguish washed over her mind, but she was uneasy feeling truly content for the first time in her life.

"Am I dead, is this purgatory, where am I?" Maya asked while seeking confirmation.

In reply, Cassandra stated with conviction, "Yes. Our creator, who brought everything into existence from a tiny speck in the midnight sky many billions of years past, put those paths on an eventual course of collision."

"What about Enum? For a while I started to believe a machine might be capable of having a personality, which I did enjoy," said Maya.

Cassandra was intrigued to find out Maya's first reaction of being in purgatory was to know what happened to Enum.

"Enum has passed too. More precisely, the artificial intelligence machine was a primary point of convergence between universes. When one of the two universes reached singularity, the final chain of events unleashed, and you happened to be stuck in the unstable one. Our creator asked me to pull you from the other reality before you faced the mortal fate."

Cassandra knew this information may be a bit overwhelming for Maya to deal with suddenly. The spirit thought perhaps a little more detail on the creator could help her understand.

The spirit continued, "As before, there are things you must now know, Maya."

A strong wind, carrying with it the smell of sage, blew across the meadow. The grasses rustled as they brushed into each other. Then, a mirage shimmered into view on the horizon, turning into a lake which hovered in the sky.

Images of various spiritual beings fade into view in the lake's waters and Cassandra disappears from the sky.

Her voice is still heard.

She continues, "There are many thousands of spirits who persist throughout all of existence. Together we form a symbiotic entity known to us as the creator. Our will is brought forth when we reach decisions as one voice. If any spirit is not in agreeance, then a result is not desired and will not manifest in the consciousness of human reality."

The waters glistened with sunlight while depicting an image of Earth rippling in tiny waves.

"This is what happened with your previous home universe, and the unstable versions, but you made a good decision. Upon creation, your own spirit did not agree to the inevitable outcome. The creator decided the outcome would be removed from existence on feasibility of a singularity, of which you helped to validate – this initiated the removal process when Enum combusted."

The image of Earth faded to nothing and the lake became flat as a sheet of glass.

"Correct decision? Validate?" Maya asked.

Cassandra responded, "Yes, however you chose in the moment, the Council trusted your decision as though you are one of us; you could say you have a kindred spirit."

Maya looked really confused now.

She blinked at Cassandra.

"Give it some time and your memories will flood back to you as they once were."

Maya blinked at Cassandra again.

"Oh, I see, your bravery really took a toll on you again. Let me give you a refresher, maybe it will help jog your memory a little, plus I really love the story," said Cassandra.

The lake electrified with thousands of tiny sparks like stars filling a midnight sky. Images of various spirits once again faded in and out of view across the top of the lake, but this time their faces animated with welcoming expressions.

"Many years before now, when reminded of Earth's inevitable situation, the Celestial Council convened to determine once and for all, if the Earth could be saved from self-destruction. You were among the spirits and volunteered yourself to action."

Cassandra moved her right arm, wrapped in long flowing silky sleeve, across the sky and an image of Maya popped into view. Maya is at the center of a crowd of Council members and they have extended their arms toward her with respect.

Small waves in the lake formed as a gentle wind picked up and whistled through the clouds.

"When you spoke up, you offered the great creator a chance to see through you as a life lived on Earth. A final decision would be made by you and we would follow through with it. Fortunately, I was able to witness your effervescence up close."

The image of Maya in the crowd morphed into an animal cell with a soft blue glow. Strangely, the cell image reminded Maya of her father when he jumped off a cliff and transformed into an orb.

"We transformed your being into a zygote and placed you inside a womb to grow. In the time leading up to your birth, memories of your past spiritual experiences dwindled to a faint reminder of something larger than yourself existing in the universe. That reminder, a feeling you could not switch off, stayed with you at all times as the pulse of your heart."

Maya started to recall some of the past, but her memory was still out of reach. Cassandra then continued as before.

"You took a risk, to become human for a generation, to prove there is another way to allow Earth to evolve without fear of singularity."

Shaking her head side to side, Maya replied to Cassandra, "I am still not so sure, if I am to be honest with you."

"There is one memory, deep in the recesses of your consciousness, which may help. I was there when your first crush turned to disappointment. You chose to become friends, unconditionally, and we remained close friends for many years. When my life was in danger, you risked your own to save me from certain death. When I told you I needed to go, you were supportive and understanding."

"Cassy?" Maya questioned.

Cassandra replied, "I know memory needs time to recover, and I do know it will recover."

"It can't be."

"Yes, sweetie. I wish that I didn't leave you alone after putting you through so much, but I knew how strong your inner spirit is, and now look at how pronounced it has become. You are a kind person on Earth who will not hesitate to do the right thing in your heart, even if it means you miss out in the process."

Maya realized then, the spirit before her was truly Cassandra. A new perception dawned on Maya, like the first time she noticed boys. She could see Cassy's younger self, older and matured in the likeliness of the spirit – her childhood best friend, grown up and beautiful.

"I will help you get back to Earth to witness the aftermath of chaos, to live throughout the next shadow, and restore you to whom you once were so that you may one day return peacefully to your spirit; it is the natural order of life."

Suddenly, with Cassandra's story of Maya's existence coming into focus, Maya understood the final words of her father.

"If the end justifies the means, how does death justify life?"

She interpreted the answer to be cyclical after it ran through her mind out of nowhere. To pass away is a literal phrase to Maya, where energy from life is passed away at death. If a person was a spirit before living, then life energy is passed back to the spirit at death. If a person was not a spirit before living, a new one is born from death. Her father, he was a spirit before living.

Images on the lake, of Maya and the crowd of spirits, faded away and the water turned placid.

A floating book materializes with a quiet hum in the air next to Maya.

"Before you return, please take the Shadow Chronicles book called into existence. Inside the works are versions of great historical events which took place on planet Earth over many thousands of years. We generated an introduction tailored to your experiences, to help you gracefully acclimate and improve memory recall."

Cassandra directs Maya's attention to the materialized book by slowly moving hand and extending a finger to point at it; her pointing digit is covered with a lacy silver flower, finger armor ring.

"The great spirits of the Council believe, as true is true, it is a right for those who restore mankind's balance to see the chronicles. Your story is added next, but you must write it in the blank pages for inclusion."

Maya gently picks up the book and swipes a hand across the sparkling cover as though she's clearing dust from the jacket. She feels a pleasant electric tingle jolt through her body as the book connects to her being for the first time.

"There is one final transformation in this process as your heroic actions are forever etched in the history of mankind. If you complete the chronicles with your entry, you will have the option to transcend life on Earth, to live forever without age."

Cassandra's statement dumbfounded Maya and she stood there, speechless, trying to digest it.

"I must go, but remember, the universe is only a thought away," said Cassandra as she faded into darkness.

Chapter 22

Celestial Council

The world around Maya melted away from a dark void dotted with twinkling stars, back to the vibrant green meadow she remembered being in after pulling Enum's lever. At first, Maya couldn't remember why she was standing in the meadow alone, but then thoughts of her encounter flooded back when she looked down to see the Chronicles book laying in the grass.

It was getting late in the day, with the sun going down over the valley. As much as Maya wanted to sleep in the meadow again, like when she was younger, she decided it was best to head back to the farmhouse.

She picked up the book and a very similar vibrating tingle happened again, like when she first brushed across the cover in purgatory. Maya believed her experience with Cassy was real, and not a dream, from the zap of static electricity.

Maya followed a beaten path through the meadow back to the farmhouse. As the sun set, a blanket of darkness enveloped the sky and covered the ground. She took a few dried logs from a wood pile next to the house on her way inside. Without electricity, due to the worldwide electromagnetic pulse, candles and a wood fire are needed provide light and warmth.

The house was a bit chilled from cool air pouring in through partially opened windows and the deer-mangled back door. Maya closed a wood storm door behind the wrecked screen door and then shut a good majority of the windows. She left one window slightly open in the living room for a breeze and to hear the katydids.

To keep things from getting too cold later in the night, Maya built a fire in the living room fireplace with the timber she brought inside. A whittling knife, several packages of long-strike matches, and rolled up newspapers are kept in a large ornate tin bucket on the floor next to a fancy cast iron log rack to help get it started. She used the knife to carve kindling and stuffed balled-up newspaper into cracks between the stacked wood.

With a fire lit, Maya grabbed her mother's cast iron teapot from the kitchen and filled it with water from a hand-pump faucet next to the sink. The pump faucet provides a backup water supply that everyone in the house knew how to use thanks to power blackouts being fairly common on the farm.

Once the kettle boiled, Maya poured a plain black tea with a portion of water. She dumped the remaining hot water into a small cast iron cooking pot with a dried bean and rice soup mix, then poured the soup into a bowl after a good stir.

Maya pulled a bar stool up to the kitchen island; with her bean and rice soup, black tea, half-loaf of French bread, and the Chronicles book placed neatly on the countertop in front of her.

The act of sitting down to a quick meal she prepared, along with countless days of too much stress, stirred an emotion deep down that Maya repeatedly refused to face. This time however, she could not refrain any longer and let the emotion take hold of her. From the pit of her stomach, it moved upward through her heart, into her mind, and out of her eyes.

Heavy tears gushed forth like a failed dam releasing a reservoir it once tirelessly held back – everything escaped together. The loss of family, running non-stop, her traumatic experiences, being alone, confusion about reality, Enum, and the end of the automated world raced through her thoughts.

She covered her eyes with her hands while squeezing her eyes shut in attempt to slow down the tears. Eventually she gave in and lived in the uncontrollable moment of emotional liberation. She felt a weight lift off her shoulders and humble for having survived everything sad and depressing she could possibly think of, but the soup and tea have lost most of their heat.

Still hungry, Maya downed the soup and a few pieces of bread. She emptied her cold into the sink and pumped more water for the kettle. Most of the fire had reduced to red-hot coals and she added a few large logs to have it burn through the night; the tea and reading would be attempted a second time.

A faint glow suddenly emanated from the book on the countertop and caught her attention. The emotional episode seemed to cause a reaction which prompted Maya's inner monologue to state it is time to read. She picked up the book, brushed her hand across to see it shimmer once again, and then opened the cover.

Written in the introductory message, "The first step to understanding everything you have been through in life is being able to confront the past honestly and without bias. This book contains a message tailored to your own experience."

"What you have witnessed is not the first or last time that Earth has nearly reached a point of singularity and mass extinction. It happened a few thousand years ago, a few thousand years before then, and it's bound to happen again."

"Human intelligence will inevitably reach a level where its concept of a civilized world breaks down and the associated confines no longer apply. Drastic measures are necessary each time, for corrective action, and the time after destruction is referred herein as a *shadow of chaos*."

Maya took a small sip of her new tea and continued reading.

"There are many shadows of chaos which demonstrate true perseverance of mankind. The electromagnetic pulse from Enum is a catastrophic event for mankind and civilization now begins a new shadow of chaos. It is a time of reflection and growth, much like plants seeding for the first time in a land scarred by a volcanic eruption."

"As shadows of chaos are understood as an overarching timeline between catastrophic events, there are also lesser timelines known as *ripples of chaos*. The ripple is a result of non-catastrophic happenings influenced by the behavior of life. For example, a person who deliberately creates a bad experience for another is sending ripples of chaos across the planet. If enough ripples collide, a river of chaos forms and grows from there."

"Over two thousand years ago, one person found singularity by leveraging extreme negativity and concentrated a spiritual practice of evil. He used power as a way to control masses of people for his own benefit, placing himself as the judge and jury, one would say. The empire went beyond creating ripples and rivers by creating waves and tsunamis of chaos."

Her eyes widened at the notion.

"Fortunately, for the benefit of mankind, a noble reached singularity before the commander of the ruthless empire could. The person leveraged humble enlightenment to destroy the empire and saved millions from disparage. Teachings of the person, who was believed to be a savior by groups of people, became a shadow of chaos and a beacon of hope for generations to follow. "

To finally know what really happened, the truth calmed Maya's mind. She questioned people about the savior at times, when they tried getting her to believe in something she couldn't fully comprehend – the answers and desperation didn't make logical sense. Politeness took over during confrontations, which helped Maya diffuse the situation with little or no ripples.

"Maya, you can create and retract ripples by thoughts alone. When you believed you could see future events by reading between the lines, you manifested real events in your subconscious. The world around you filled with illusions you create, but those illusions become realities to the rest of the world. As in the meaning of the name, Maya, a Hindu goddess of illusion."

"Try to imagine chaotic ripples as vectors in the concept of Cause and Effect. While an action generates a series of resulting actions, chaotic ripples are the path in which consequence travels. They radiate outward from the cause like sound waves and pool together to form an effect."

"You found singularity by thought process alone, while your father reached it using computer programs. This most recent event is the first time where more than one person found singularity in such a short span of time. We know he aided you to the anti-algorithm, which only expedited things, but you were on pace to find it regardless."

In the moment, Maya realized the feeling lingering throughout her entire life, as it's meant to be understood. Her existence, now vindicated, is no longer plagued by nagging animosity, doubt, or uncertainty established through her perception of the world.

She wept as her mind released itself from an impenetrable grip on depression and toxicity. Her tears escaped like steam from a pressure valve cracked open for the first time in years.

"I don't know the half of it," Maya said to her mind and then smiled with content.

Throughout her life, Maya struggled with exclusion, which she now realizes as an inevitable consequence of living because of chaotic ripples. Despite feeling indifferent and disconnected from others, she is no longer confused or excluded and feels indemnified in understanding she is part of something larger than imagination could perceive – and fortunate to have that existence confirmed to her personally.

***

Maya took a break from reading the book for two reasons. One, the content overwhelmed her like past conversations with her father. The other reason was out of her control, as the world suddenly faded to black like she witnessed before when Enum sent her to alternate universes.

Similar to her experiences traveling inside wormholes, Maya floated down a tunnel toward a tiny circle of light in the distance. Approaching the white speck reminded her of sulfur ignition from lighting an entire book of matches on fire at once. The matchbook intensely burned tiny and bright, but then quickly filled her field of vision as she raced closer and closer to a point of no return.

As she floated through the tunnel, the soft voice of Cassandra resonated.

"The best way to understand the Celestial Council is by looking at their guidance as derived from experience on Earth. Members of the Council each provided a path forward for humanity in the most trying times of history. They possess strong traits of defining positivity and hope, but are far from perfect shining examples of morality."

The wormhole spat Maya out on Earth, in the middle of an empty Lexton city intersection at night. She felt awake and clairvoyant, but also felt confused and discombobulated from the journey – the world she knew had changed dramatically.

Horse-drawn carriages transported people and goods down deteriorating asphalt streets that vehicles once dominated. Oil braziers lit corners of intersections and handheld torches helped people find their way at night. Without electric, the world was forced to find new ways to exist by using old technology.

Anything with a circuit was fried when the electromagnetic pulse blasted across the planet. It was a force so powerful that the shockwave rippled through the Earth's crust and effectively rendered underground bunkers, built to protect electronics, as useless. Even expertly crafted Faraday cages did not stand a chance against the powerful surge of feedback.

People across the world, who depended on electricity to survive day-to-day, needed to work together to overcome the sudden change. It was not any easy progression by any means. Violence and hysteria plagued the world unlike any other time in history, even greater than being at ground-zero in the world wars.

Equipment dependent on active electricity was repurposed for building materials, barricades, and projectiles in the immediate aftermath. Thus, people who were lost by absence of technology used lifeless technology in attempt to destroy each other's lives; large amounts proprietary knowledge was lost along the way, repeating like the burning of Alexandria's great library.

Once anger among people subsided, they felt happier than they did in their lives filled with electronics. The days are longer and more fulfilling with a much larger portion of time requiring physical activity. People became less lazy with communication and appreciated the effort of others more than before the blackout.

Yet, it was strictly Maya's perception which generalized that many people were happy after the Armageddon of electronics. While a vast number of people did find relief in an age of peace, a large percentage became increasingly frustrated. They banded together to start a brutal uprising against complacency that would last for years to come.

The council, though relieved that humanity dodged singularity once again, became concerned over the uprising on Earth. Throughout the entire history of mankind, revolutions by like-minded individuals are common, but the latest involved millions of people with a fair amount of residual knowledge and technology retained from before the change.

Scientists and engineers postulated several different theories for what happened and pointed the finger at a giant, nearby cosmic event, such as a supernova implosion triggering intense radiation to bombard and disable electronics on Earth. In all technicality, their theories weren't too far from the truth.

Groups of people, who were unhappy about being set back to the dark ages desperately craved to reinvent computers and build them with more power and stability than before – they wanted a new breed of electronics capable of surviving the anything the random universe could conjure.

Ironically, proponents of newly advanced electronics did not realize or understand it was a computer that put them into their very situation to begin with. For a few centuries, the devices created with unending hours of human ingenuity and persistence eroded people from the inside to the point of uncontrollable isolation and greed.

Chapter 23

Earth Beyond

A beacon of hope is among the wreckage of a world once relieved of computerized technology, and it's an entirely new way of thinking. Rather than resorting to competitiveness, people moved to ritualistically practice inclusivity. The mantra, no person left behind, turned into reality through and through without prejudice.

After near-extinction of all life on Earth, a vast population realized a different approach to living is needed to survive the next catastrophic event – a principal belief ruling the world nearly a hundred years after the apocalyptic event. The people of Earth established an insurance plan for mankind as a whole and proactively built a new future in control of destiny.

Upon her arrival in the post-technology world, Maya walked into an empty street tavern lit by ornate sconces similar to those she noticed in the Station Seven bunker. She thought she could talk to someone and clear up her confusion.

Nobody was around to help. She was about to search elsewhere when she spotted a strange book laying on the tavern bar. The book jacket was solid dark purple with the title of 'Earth Beyond' printed in large, plain gold Roman letters, with the author name in a smaller font below, Felix Ordell.

Intrigued by the simple lettering and one-color background, Maya picked the book up and skimmed through; thinking it might be another Celestial Council storybook for her.

She attempted to make the book glisten by brushing her hand across the cover, but there was no otherworldly response this time - no shimmer or sparkle in the light, or feeling of energy pulsing through her body. She was not overwhelmed by its presence, or captivated like hold a gift from god, yet she felt a need to read it.

The author talked about his moral compass in an unassuming way and described a notion of how he believes the world could change for the better with the right motivation. He emphasized theoretical physics and how humanity's progress is not sustainable as it is.

The notion, which evolved new civilization, originated from the deep-thinking author shortly after Enum's electromagnetic pulse. As a respected philosopher, Ordell suggested that to overcome great unknowns of the universe, people need to help each other on a global project. He called the ambitious initiative, Earth Beyond, named for a principal goal of the project – to go beyond Earth.

To achieve success with the global project, mankind would need to reinvent computers, and electricity, with a primary purpose of powering navigation and survival systems needed to aid life beyond the planet. The new technology would be designated to the project only and not intended for personal use.

With existing equipment, enough residual knowledge, and determination to attain a better destiny for mankind, the world transformed once again. People worked together to rebuild from the rubble by resurrecting electricity and computers.

Oddly enough, even with prior expertise, it still required roughly the same amount of time to rebuild, from steam to nuclear, as it did to invent the technologies the first time. Since mankind had adapted very well to rebuilding from destruction from natural disasters in the past, they were up for the challenge this time.

Ordell's philosophy meant people putting differences aside in order to fulfill a purpose larger than themselves, for future survival of the human species. He created plans for space vessels the size of countries, known as Earth Arks, to advance mankind into the cosmos for once and all. Every person would be included to help and travel if they wish, while societal structure provided incentive.

From a technical standpoint, Earth Arks are fairly complex lattice structures, each made by attaching thousands of independent modules to form a much larger object. The modules are sent to space as rocket payloads and fixed to a growing superstructure orbiting the Earth.

Every module has a primary function, like a living quarters, kitchen, sick bay, or research lab as examples. There are plans for construction bays designed to build replacement modules in space, as well as plans for microclimates and Earth-like ecosystems. With enough time and modules, it's possible the superstructure would eventually grow to the size of a planet, provided enough resources are obtained throughout its journey in space.

Once an Earth Ark reached a certain size, thruster bays are activated and the ship is pushed further out into space to escape Earth's gravity and prevent it from falling back to the surface. By the time Maya arrived, ten combined Earth Arks with millions of people onboard exist in the staging area just past the gravitational field.

Felix knew that immediate generations of the civilized world would have difficulty adjusting to a new philosophical way of life needed to attain his ultimate vision, but he viewed the adjustment as only a small and temporary barrier to success. By removing common burdens of everyday life, each individual would truly be free to contribute to the global effort.

One phrase from his notes reads as, "If the entire world of people were working on a common goal together, they would lift each other up and no one person would be left behind. They would help, not only because everyone is helping, but through the desire of others wanting them to help."

His notes continued, "With one goal shared among all people of the planet, commerce is not needed and greed shall fade into darkness where it belongs. All resources on the planet put toward attaining this goal will both facilitate and nourish those who contribute."

A divide remained between those unwilling to participate and the pioneers of galactic travel. Felix predicted independent populations would break away from the common goal and stated that people will do as they will. He didn't ostracize and instead accommodated their choice by proposing only those who contribute may travel.

Maya wasn't sure what to make of the text, knowing how prone Ordell's idea is to slavery and manipulation. She didn't believe it at first, to have billions of people share a common vision, until she read his next passage.

"Over ninety percent of the world believes in some sort of spiritual existence. What if survival of the near destruction of our planet is a sign from life beyond, from the gods above, that everyone is subject to extermination by nature regardless of what they believe?"

"By quake, or volcano, hurricane, landslide, typhoon, tsunami, tornado, or an asteroid from space, we cannot have chance. Nature might be our mother, but her increasing and destructive forces are telling us it's time to leave the nest."

Ordell then punctuated his point.

"We can learn to travel the universe and survive to keep our beliefs alive, or we can stand still and let nature consume us back into dust."

"Natural processes are only disasters when they affect human life, or supporting life humans care about which enables them to live. Nature does not discriminate and can take anyone's life in an instant without remorse."

The hair on the back of Maya's neck jolted and she felt a tingling sensation. In that moment, she seen Ordell's message as clear as optical fiber.

Anyone can believe what they want, and humans know Earth will not think or believe otherwise, but instead carry out actions as it's designed to do.

Earth Beyond resonated with millions and millions around the globe rather rapidly. In the beginning, before Ordell's work was well known, enough people believed in his message to recreate printing presses to distribute copies of the book worldwide. To many, he achieved what was long considered as impossible, to unite the people of Earth for the common good.

Incidentally, printing presses were selected as the primary distribution method of the message because they had the lowest impact on resources required by his vision. Presses didn't need extra equipment to receive a message like broadcasting, or a global internet communication system.

Within two decades after Felix passed away from old age, his writting transformed a wayward world into a planet of purpose. People participated in his vision for a chance to become space pioneers instead of infighting. Everything as promised was provided because everyone worked together and shared Ordell's dream.

Maya needed to see it. She couldn't believe the revolution she read about actually happened after the world went dark from her actions. The very thought caused her to spiral backward to a depressive way of thinking.

She put the Earth Beyond book back on the bar and walked outside. The streets were barren as before, not a soul in sight, but she noticed a large amber glow on the horizon between two vacant apartment buildings. It looked like a fire engulfing an entire forest in the distance and a feeling inside beckoned her closer.

Every ten to twenty minutes on her walk, Maya would see a series of bright lights followed by pillars of smoke reaching upward, emanating from the area. After the first time seeing what looked like rocket launches, she thought Ordell's philosophy became reality.

The reinvention of rocket technology only needed to account for leaving Earth's atmosphere with a payload to a specified coordinate. Since the rocket itself would not return, research on reentry was unnecessary at the time. Earth Ark clusters in space would pull the entire rocket in, extract the module and people, then repurpose the material.

Two hours, and hundreds of rockets, went by as Maya walked toward the flickering glow before getting close enough to identify the source. She walked up a small hill next to the road to watch discretely with hope of not being noticed.

A flurry of activity in a clearing was taking place, lit by torches and burning barrels. Multiple welders were tacking metal to module walls while electricians wired up the inside. Cranes on tracks distributed material to module stations, allowing work to continue uninterrupted. When a module was completed, it was moved off the assembly line and trucked to one of several launchpads.

It was strange for Maya, to see a number of people working together like a well-oiled machine. Food trucks zipped around the clearing, delivering meals with beverages to workers; a stark contrast from a truck parked on a street corner waiting for patrons to approach it.

The workers were like zombies, focused on a single directive and nearly oblivious to the world around them. While pitched as free will, Ordell's message appeared like brainwashing in action, but it was deceiving from a distance. The reason being, people were free of burden and no longer plagued their minds with worry, hate, or greed.

***

"Cassandra, I need your help. I fear people are leaving the planet," Maya said.

As promised, Cassy returned to Earth and appeared before Maya as an apparition on the hill within a few minutes.

While smiling, Cassandra replied, "Indeed, they are. Humans have finally learned to move past petty differences and work together – they are trying to find the Council."

Maya felt an overwhelming sensation wash over her entire being, which could be described as a mixture of contentedness, warmth, and glee. She transformed into a ball of blue light floating on the hill top, free from the bounds of gravity.

www.ingramcontent.com/pod-product-compliance
Lightning Source LLC
Chambersburg PA
CBHW051952240626
47153CB00005B/1720